CHIMERA

From the window of your soul
Look out over the sea of experience and expectation
Towards the island of reason
Where grows the chimeric tree of knowledge
With its fruits of creativity
And beyond to the pinnacles of achievement
Where the winged messengers fly.

Enid M. Smith

CHIMERA

Edited by Jan Slade

PARTHIAN

Parthian
The Old Surgery
Napier Street
Cardigan
SA43 1ED

www.parthianbooks.co.uk

First published in 2009
© the authors 2009
All Rights Reserved

ISBN 978-1-905762-71-2

Editor: Jan Slade

Cover image by Enid Smith
Design & typesetting by www.lucyllew.com
Printed and bound by Dinefwr Press, Llandybïe, Wales

Published with the financial support of the Welsh
Books Council

British Library Cataloguing in Publication Data

A cataloguing record for this book is available from
the British Library

CONTENTS

MIRAGE

INFINITY

FOREWORD

The chimera: from Greek mythology a fire breathing hybrid of lion, goat and serpent; any fabulous creature made up from the body part of various animals; a (grotesque) product of the imagination.

From the Plato of *The Republic* to the oppressive regimes of the twentieth century – some of which haunt the fringes of this collection – authority figures of all kinds have been anxious to censor writers because of their ability not only to imagine (in Plato's terms to lie), but, through imagination, to expose the monstrosity and the deep human truths that these very authorities would seek to deny. In this sense, the ten contributors to the playfully named *Chimera*, all students on the MA in Creative Writing at Trinity University College Carmarthen, are in good company. They share with the French philosopher, Pascal, who knew a thing or two about the power of thinking and writing down the unthinkable, an awareness that, despite (or perhaps because of) the dictionary definitions, people are the most chimeric thing in existence. They all share his view: 'What a chimera then is man! What a novelty! What a monster, what a chaos, what a contradiction, what a prodigy! Judge of all things, feeble earthworm, depository of truth, a sink of uncertainty and error, the glory and the shame of the universe.'

Here, there are stories and poems by Jan Slade, Enid Smith and Jo Perkins which rewrite the material of Greek, Christian, Celtic and other mythologies; playfully re-imagining the chimeric Serpent of the Garden of Eden as a kind of fashion consultant, the myth of the chimera in terms of office politics, and dragons as the stuff of childhood imagination.

Other stories confront the notion of transformation more bleakly. Sarah Tanner writes of the cyborg world – no longer just the stuff of imagination – in which the human becomes part of the machine, losing its very humanity; and, in a truly beautiful piece, of a prince and princess not allowed any simple happy ever after. Similarly, but stylistically very differently, Jo Perkins and Enid Smith dare to imagine the unimaginable in confronting the reality of death.

Death too, and more generally the precariousness of life, is a concern of Lucy Delbridge and Caroline James in both poetry and prose. Both imagine individuals transformed, not by the mechanisms of myth or the brutality of technology, but by the fragility of their own bodies and the ways in which medical intervention might be both necessary but equally grotesque in denying other freedoms and other dreams. Like all the writers here, each in her own way, they explore the paradox exemplified in Pascal's sense of humans as both 'the glory and shame of the universe'. They re-imagine for us in Jones' memorable phrase the 'Hate, lust, torture / Teasing and tantalising in / The stillness.' And with lust there is also love.

In a more down to earth way Jan Slade's Satan reminds us that in all considerations of the chimeric nature of the human 'sex has got a lot to answer for'; and sex figures here both directly and more subtly. This is particularly true of the exquisitely realised monologues and multi-perspective narratives by Katy Griffiths, who shares with Jessica Ledbetter, Penny Sutton and Perkins, and the poetry of Llinos Jones, an interest in the exploration of the secrets – sometimes monstrous, sometimes mundane, sometimes both – of all human relationships. Secrets exist in the hidden lives of apparently attractive partners who turn out to be conmen, of those forced to deny sexual and other kinds of abuse, and in words unspoken or family histories untold or not believed. Sutton reminds us: the serpent is always in the garden, the abuser in apparent paradise. As Jones suggests, in the midst of the possibility of love we also feel the sharpness, the cutting edge, of 'dead confetti of open shells underfoot'.

This is writing interested in the limitations of the imagination in the modern world, and the pervasiveness of lies of various kinds (captured in Ledbetter's 'silicone world' and botox tears of LA, as much as in Perkins' Auschwitz). Yet, like all the contributors here, Griffiths and Ledbetter celebrate the power of the imagination to transform that world: in an aunt's ability to tell fanciful stories which turn out to be true, or the child-like insistence that we should all forget our adult selves and 'stand in the rain'.

We might feel that Plato has won: that writers have been expelled from the Republic as at best not much use and at worst dangerous liars; that we no longer allow for the possibilities of the chimera. But this writing in all its variety suggests that there is still room in our world for humorous, troubling and dangerous imaginative writing. It is in this sense a truly fabulous and chimeric collection.

Paul Wright

CREATION

A Modern Myth

Jo Perkins

Jackie looked around the newsroom and wondered if it had been a good idea to come back to work after all. The job was straightforward enough but she wasn't sure whether the wages were adequate compensation for having to endure the office politics. She looked unhappily down at the pile of newspaper cuttings about the current crisis in the Middle East, that straggled across her desk.

About her, ageing hacks dozed, one eye half focused on the computer screens in front of them, the other absent-mindedly scanning the room for unusual events. Every now and again they would rouse themselves for the sport of baiting the newly trained young things whose enthusiasm was as keen as the ironed edges on their shirtsleeves. Their advancing years and prodigious consumption of drink stopped them from remembering just how unpleasant it was to be a novice in this most competitive of professions.

Fran sat frowning at the computer terminal next to her. She was trying to work out why a large sum of money had disappeared from her bank account. Fran had shown her where to sit and put her coat the first day. Jackie liked Fran, a bit. She trusted her, a little. Fran had a man, she knew that much, but she wasn't the type with whom you could sit and discuss the absorbability of disposable nappies or whether to try terry ones or not. Fran had worked here for years and was hanging on for a short while longer to bulk up her redundancy payment so that it would amount to a deposit on a decent little place in France. Fran was interested in work, drink and grown up fun. But at least she'd been decent enough to warn her about Kay, she could have let her fall straight into her clutches.

At the far end of the room, beyond the rows of pale wood desks and monitors, Jackie could just see Kay. About her desk she had created a jungle of plants that she had bought from the shop next to the railway station. She watched as Kay pushed her thick blonde hair behind her ears and shuffled papers. Kay was something of a legend in the business. She dominated this little empire. She could destroy people's careers and indeed sometimes had. She made it her business to know every detail of her workers' personal circumstances and just how close they were teetering to the edge of bankruptcy. She was happy to simper and flirt meekly in front of the bosses, but equally, she relished the chance to verbally maul her victims in front of a hostile audience. Kay was in charge of the newsroom, the important parts such as expenses and overtime. The other business, of the production of news, was left to those still sober enough or riddled with ambition. All of a sudden Kay looked up, directly at her. Jackie shuddered at the intensity of Kay's gaze and slithered back out of her sight behind the computer.

A man, whom Jackie had not seen before, strode into the room. Tall and good looking, with blond curly hair and the sort of physique that is not acquired by drinking fifteen pints every Friday night. Several scores of eyes watched his progress without apparently losing interest in the vitally urgent work on their computer screens.

'Who's he?' Jackie asked Fran.

'Who's the Greek god that's just walked into the room?'

Fran looked across the room myopically, her eyes slow to adjust from dodgy debit to passing poppet.

'Oh, that's Mark. He's just been kicked out of Features. Most people thought it was because he spent too much time admiring himself in the mirror, but it wasn't. His boss fancied him, Mark wouldn't play her games and she got her frumpy middle aged knickers in a twist. Then she put in a claim for sexual harassment. The managing director gave him a formal warning and he's been sent to us in Siberia as a punishment. I think they're rather hoping Kay will finish him off.'

'Fancy a drink after work?'

A wave of aftershave lapped around Jackie's desk, anaesthetising her from the rest of the room while she dealt with the problem in front of her. The problem sat on the corner of her desk swinging a rather short leg. It ended in a dapper black boot and a stacked heel. Between the end of the trousers and the boot was a scarily pale section of hairy leg.

'Er, no thanks,' Jackie replied, 'I have a train to catch.'

She would have said this even if this had not been true. She had no intention of having her evening hijacked by a balding middle aged no hoper, even if he did have a bit of a way with words and a very small amount of charm.

'Maybe another time then.'

Or maybe not, thought Jackie.

The problem hopped off her desk and went away.

Jackie immersed herself in the problems of the Middle East for a time in an attempt to block out some of the oddballs surrounding her. There seemed little chance of peace and harmony in either place. Even though she was working part time and could step back as an impartial observer, Jackie was still interested in the mechanics of the office politics. An information gathering expedition might not be a bad idea. She collected together a few important looking pieces of paper and set off on a purposeful meander across the room. She edged her way around people lounging in front of their computers; some were busy with coffee and newspapers, others deep in personal administration. A few looked up briefly as she passed just to make sure she was not checking up on them. She wandered past the glass boxes which housed the bosses; they were filling their time as fruitfully as their employees, but in better quality suits.

Then across her path came the Greek god bearing a pile of newspaper cuttings and personal effects. He gave her a broad but largely synthetic smile which vanished when he realised that she wasn't anyone important. He sighed and dumped his possessions on an empty desk in front of Kay's jungle.

'Jackie can I have you for a minute please!' Kay's voice cut through the foliage.

How the hell did she see me through all that, Jackie thought. She wondered which one of Kay's legendary sides she was going to be treated to. Would it be the benign one, would she be aggressive or just caustic? Today the outlook was good.

Close up Kay was older than she expected – no one under forty had hair that colour. She filled most of her ergonomically designed office chair, which she twisted round effortlessly to face Jackie.

'How are you settling in? They're very happy with your work, do you want any extra shifts?'

'Well yes, please,' Jackie lied, although Kay did not seem to be expecting an answer from her. Jackie would have preferred to work less in this inhospitable newsroom, but a vision of her mortgage advisor floated through her head and convinced her that she was forming the correct answer to Kay's question.

'While you think about it, can you fill in your bank details on this.'

As she passed the form across to Jackie, it caught on the identity card which hung round her neck, setting it dancing on its long chain.

The conversation seemed to be over, so Jackie headed back to her desk.

'That woman,' she said to Fran, 'that woman is very strange. She has what sounds like an Asian name but she's blonde and she has an unusual accent.'

'Well, we can't all be Australians,' Fran replied.

7

Jackie was beginning to think that Kay was not one of Fran's favourite subjects of conversation, but Fran continued,

'I think she's from Turkey originally, but she's been in this country for years. Perhaps she anglicised her name to Meerah, makes it easier for us to remember her. She scares most of us witless.'

The two women watched as Kay approached Mark, who was setting up camp at his new desk. Some sort of altercation was taking place.

'This is going to be interesting,' Fran said.

'Not only has Mark been made to sit at the naughty desk next to Kay, but they're arguing already. I suppose he's put in one of his flamboyantly creative expenses claims.'

Mark turned towards them, they could see his face was flushed with anger. He took his coat and headed off noisily towards the door.

'I expect the management's told him to go out, hunt down, kill and cook an exclusive ready for tomorrow. Better that than being Kay's punchbag,' Fran mused, before returning her attention to her bank account.

It was some days before Jackie was in work again. The arrangement suited her perfectly. She had enough time in the real world to be able to readjust and treat the inmates of the newsroom with the contempt and possibly the sympathy that they deserved. A delayed train had made her late and she rushed across the road from the station, dodged the cars that were dithering for a space in the car park and made her way to the back door of the office block. Rather surprisingly there were two police officers standing outside.

Perhaps a royal visit or a photo opportunity for some

jumped up politician, Jackie thought as she searched in her bag for her identity card. She walked past the policemen towards the door; they swiftly and professionally stepped in her path.

'Your ID please,' one of them said. He inspected Jackie's card.

'And where do you work?'

'In the newsroom. Is someone important visiting?'

'No, not at all, unless you count the forensic bunch as royalty,' the second policeman replied, obviously relishing his position of superiority even if it was only in the 'significant things that I know and you don't department'.

'Why, what's happened?' Jackie asked, beginning to realise that this was not the start of an ordinary working day.

'Oh, I'm afraid we can't tell you that,' the first policeman said helpfully.

Jackie went up the back staircase to the newsroom. As she entered the long corridor she ran straight into a bunch of her colleagues. Heads swivelled towards her and back again. Looking for a familiar face she spotted Fran lounging nonchalantly against a wall.

'Why are you all out here, what's going on? Have I missed something?'

Fran jerked her head towards the glass partition that kept the newsroom out of the corridor. Through the window Jackie saw the figures of the forensic team stepping carefully through a maze of mashed houseplants.

'They say we can go back inside in five minutes. They've nearly finished collecting evidence. Mark went a bit crazy last night. Yesterday, he'd been sent out on some near on impossible stories, he'd managed to come back with the goods but then Kay started on him about his expenses. He went out on some massive bender, God knows what he'd been taking but he came back in here late yesterday evening, completely out of it, found Kay still at her desk and...'

'Can I have your attention please!' The suit that was rarely seen outside his glass box raised his voice in the crowded corridor.

'We all know what happened here yesterday, it's been a very messy business but this is the sort of time when we must all pull together and get back into our stride straight away. Most importantly,' he looked knowingly over his spectacles at the crowd, 'I don't want to find myself reading about this in the gossip columns of the national press. You can return to your desks now.'

Jackie filed into the newsroom with the others, reflecting that she appeared to be the only one in the building who did not know what had happened. The area around Kay's desk was taped off, her chair lay on its back and the plants were strewn around. Every drawer of her filing cabinet and desk had been emptied on to the floor.

Jackie dropped her bag on her desk and turned to Fran. 'So what happened next?'

'Oh, yes,' Fran realised she was mid story, 'apparently Mark started accusing her of all sorts, most of which was true I expect. Manipulating people's personnel files, fiddling payments, that sort of thing. He started looking for evidence in her files because she wasn't daft enough to keep things like that on her computer. She screams blue murder and security arrives, but not before Mark finds her private records of information about people, that they really wouldn't want to be made public. Including some particularly juicy facts about the head honcho here.'

'So why were the police brought in?' Jackie asked.

'Cos Kay was alleging assault and Mark had that previous little problem. Security panicked '

'So is Mark going to be charged? Did he hit her?' asked Jackie.

'Nope, he didn't touch her. The management turned up as well and Mark told them what he'd found. They were so appalled and embarrassed to find out what Kay had been doing, there are rumours about blackmail, probably about themselves. He's come out of it smelling sweet, Kay's been suspended, without pay, and will no doubt lose her job. There's talk of criminal charges, the police have been taking away documents and Mark's back as golden boy again.'

'So, that's the end of Kay, poor woman, her career gone.'

'Poor woman!' Fran snorted. 'Kay Meerah was a monster.'

In Storage

Llinos Jones

I'll pluck out the
stars from my eyes, the shimmer
that once meant something at some time,
roll them up like tacky fairy lights
store them corroding in the attic
and forget.

I'll pack up
my dreams, these delicate things,
formed of wishes and delusion,
bubble-wrap
their brittleness with care
tuck them, light-fingered,
in safe shelters
and hope.

And I'll take back my heart
please
to tape up its scuffed exterior
soothe its bruised tenderness
and keep it until
the next time.

The Truth

Jan Slade

Well, hello-o. Sso nicce to ssee you. Ssuch pleassure to have a vissitor, not many people bother thesse dayss.

Oh, you're from The Eden Newss, and want to hear about Them you ssay? Well, I'm jusst the persson, I've been wanting to have my ssay for a long time now. Righto, assk away.

My name? Oh, I've lotss of namess, not all of them nicce, but in the 'casst lisst', sso to ssay, I appear ass 'The Sserpent,' but you can call me Nick.

Right, let me sset the record sstraight.

Sshe wass ssuch a lovely girl, young and innossent, sshe used to come and ssit... Oh look, this is ridiculous, would you mind awfully if I dropped the accent? Those sibilants are such hard work and I only do it for effect. Supposed to make me sound sinister or something. Stupid idea!

Anyway, where was I? Oh yes, Eve.

As I say she was very pleasant, always had a friendly word, used to sit with me for hours whenever she wanted to get away from *him*.

Mmm, *him*. All that 'dominion over the creatures that crawl on the earth and inhabit the sky' stuff went to his head. Strutted around like the lord of all he surveyed, giving his orders, even to her, poor thing. It was 'Eve, do this,' 'Eve do that,' 'Eve fetch this,' 'Eve carry that,' all day long. She never had a moment's peace when he was around.

That's why she spent so much time with me, of course. She used to sit on a branch with me coiled round it – and round her too sometimes – talking about this and that. You know, who was doing what with whom, what the rabbits were getting up to, the meaning of life, that sort of thing. Ooh, and fashion. That's how she started playing around with the leaves and things, putting a flower in her hair, or making a necklace out of leaves and berries. Suited her, I must say, she was a beautiful girl. Mind, it got a bit out of hand when she found the fig leaves. You know what they say, the more you cover up the more interesting you become. Well, that was the start of it really. That and the rabbits. She asked me what it was exactly that they were doing and, of course, I told her. Well I didn't see any harm in it; it was going on all over the place after all. She didn't understand at first, and it took me *ages* to explain. I can see her now, thoughtfully chewing on an apple, and then the penny dropped. She looked at me in horror, her face all red and teary.

'Oh, that's disgusting!' she cried. 'I could never do that!'

'Just as well, Ducky,' I said. 'Hasn't the Landlord put a

clause in the lease, forbidding it? No, Deary, you just forget all about it. Ooh,' I added, trying to change the subject, 'doesn't that blackberry look nice, just there, where you've put it?' But she'd gone all quiet. She left soon after that and I didn't see her for days, then she suddenly turned up, sobbing her heart out.

'Oh, Beelzebub,' she cried (her little pet name for me, you know), 'oh, Beelzebub, I'm so miserable. He won't leave me alone. He's on at me all the time and I can't stand it any more. What am I going to do?'

Well, it turned out she'd gone and told him about the bloody rabbits, silly cow. I was so cross I could have stamped my feet.

Eh? ...What do you mean, no feet? Oh, yes, but you know what I mean. Anyway, don't interrupt.

Once he got the idea into his head he wouldn't let it drop. It was pester, pester, pester all day long. 'Course, in the end she gave in. Apparently he pulled rank on her – you know, 'I was here first,' 'I'm older than you,' 'It's my garden and you'll do what I say,' that kind of thing. And he *sulked*. Need I say more? The first I knew of it was when I next saw him; big cheesy grin, extra bit of swagger in his strut, smug look on his face. Git!

Anyway, he made such a big deal of it, boasting to all and sundry, that the Landlord got to hear of it. Well, was *He* angry! Down He comes in a thunderbolt, all billowing clouds and sound FX, very Star Wars! Ranting and raving about broken clauses and threatening all sorts of reprisals. She was ever so upset, kept saying she felt so ashamed and was really sorry, and in the end she ran off – right out of the garden!

15

As for that Adam, slimy sod, – well he blamed it on *her*, would you believe.

'Oh, Your High and Mightiness', he grovelled. 'She made me do it, Sir. She was gagging for it, Your Reverence, dressed in all those leaves and flowers, and as for that blackberry! Bit of a slut if you ask me, Your Eminence.'

Now I'll say this for Him Upstairs, He doesn't like crawlers. (Well, you've only got to look at me.) Anyway, He pointed His Finger and Proclaimed:

'Shut up! I will hear no more. You've sinned and that's that. You've got responsibilities now. What if she becomes a Mother? You will leave the Garden and find her and cherish her. And until you learn to treat her with respect you are banished forever. Now sod off.'

And with that he was gone, with a great big POUF!

Adam just stood there, quivering with fear and whimpering, then he noticed me.

'It's all *your* fault,' he snivelled.

'Don't you start on me,' I told him. '*I* didn't invent it. No,' I said, 'and neither did you, you nasty little worm, though you seemed to think so, the way you carried on once you'd got your own way.' Ooh, I was so cross! 'And as for all that blaming her, that's evil, that is. I thought *I* was supposed to be the nasty one around here, but you take the biscuit. Now, trot along, little boy,' I sneered, 'and do what Daddy told you to,' and with that I gave him one of my looks, turned my back on him and left him to it.

Well, that's about all there is to it really. He was just like all men, chasing after it as if his life depended on it, then when he gets it, he thinks he's doing the *woman* a favour. Makes me spit! And he obviously didn't learn his lesson 'cos they never came back, and the Garden became a ruin. I was made redundant, and that's why I'm here in this dreadful Home for the Fallen.

Sex has got a lot to answer for, if you ask me.

Damien Dime

Jo Perkins

Damien Dime's name was not the one he had been born with but it was one which he thought would take him to the top. His life so far looked good on paper, uncluttered with spouse, children or mortgage. He felt it would be difficult for job interviewers to deny him the position he coveted.

The fact was though, his life was also unencumbered with friends, relations and the truth.

The need for bits of paper to prove his life so far had not presented any problems with the development of sophisticated colour copiers. But his application for the post of Sales Director at the prodigiously young age of twenty-six, as well as raising eyebrows among his resentful colleagues, had caused him some concern. His Cambridge first was no surprise to those he worked with, his long abandoned family would have been more surprised.

For at the age of eighteen, on the day he received confirmation of his place at Cambridge, his father walked out on his family for a much younger woman, who also happened to be the teenage Damien's girlfriend. Without the money to support him at university and tortured by his girlfriend's betrayal, Damien turned his back on his family and early life and got a job cleaning aeroplanes. When he wearied of clearing away the detritus of long haul flights, he took to selling, a job he did well, not having ever felt the need to be truthful.

The application for the post of Sales Director presented the problem of creating the highly ornate embossed document establishing his degree. His phone call to the two line ad in the evening paper resolved the dilemma. He wrote to the forger with the essential details, using a colleague's computer terminal and carefully eradicating all trace of his document.

The call to his boss' office was not really a surprise. He had expected to discuss the job application with him further, but when he was confronted with the document he had sent to 'Instant Awards' the previous day, Damien Dime thought it was probably time to look for another job. A computer boffin employed solely to uncover corporate misdemeanours had spotted the document in the depths of the computer's limbo land and passed it on to his boss.

The letter confirming the reasons for his dismissal arrived as Damien was wondering whether it was time to change his name again. For his next job, he'd gone back to the familiar tarmac of the airport as an air marshall. He enjoyed the power he had over the massive jumbos, slotting them into their parking spaces with one flap of his table tennis bat.

But Damien was not one for standing still. He filled in his new job application form deftly, slotting in dates and places. The ink on the two references was nearly dry. Damien wondered whether he should have given himself a few more years of job experience as a junior at Heathrow. After all, the job of senior air traffic controller was going to be a very demanding one.

Upgraded

Sarah Tanner

The pain was beyond anything he had ever experienced.

Hovering on the cusp of consciousness, but never allowed to sink into welcome oblivion, he was aware of voices, of cold hands in latex gloves, soft-tipped pens drawing on his skin, needles sinking into his flesh, the blades of scalpels sinking through skin, muscles, tendons, organs and bones.

How long it lasted he never knew, only that the pain felt as if it had always been a part of him, as if it would never end. There was no way to count the passing time for there was no night, no day, and he was never allowed to sleep. Drugs were pumped into his paralysed body, dulling the pain enough to keep him alive, keeping him awake but unable to move, aware but unable to speak.

Another needle was thrust into his arm, and he felt the flood of drugs flushing through his veins. Gradually, the paralysis begin to recede.

He blinked, a bright light shining in his eyes. He tried to moan in pain, but was unable to do more than move his lips soundlessly.

A face, covered with a white surgical mask and cap with goggles over the eyes, appeared in his line of vision. The rest of the body was clothed in a white coat and wearing latex gloves.

'Subject XT743 has regained consciousness,' it said, its voice human but genderless. 'XT743 is the first of the XT model to have regained consciousness.' The face leaned forwards and waved a finger in front of his eyes. 'Subject appears at least partially aware and is responding to visual stimuli.' It paused, then said, 'Can you hear me?'

He managed a weak nod.

'Subject XT743 is responding to audible stimuli.'

He opened his mouth and tried to speak again, but no sound came out.

'Subject XT743 is attempting communication,' the figure observed, 'and whilst unable to speak, this suggests coherent thought processes. We must cross-reference with other XT subjects to ascertain whether this is a single occurrence or consistent with the recovery of all XT models.'

He found he could move his fingers and tried to lift his arm, but his body wouldn't obey him. His muscles refused to cooperate. He managed a weak gasp before giving up.

Another figure came into focus, this one clearly female. 'Fascinating,' she said and leaned closer. 'And he was the most difficult to upgrade. Maybe he'll actually be worth the trouble. Keep me updated on every XT's recovery, but especially this one.'

Both figures disappeared, the sound of their footsteps quietly receded, followed by the hiss of an automatic door. He was left alone again.

Some time later, more people dressed like the first figure entered the room. They did not speak. They made him sit up and lie back down, moving his arms and legs carefully, moving every joint, over and over again as if they were a series of exercises he needed to go through.

It hurt. Every movement ached and hurt. He could barely lift his arms or legs, which all felt oddly heavy and cumbersome. He winced and mumbled in pain, and speech was still painful.

One of the figures forced his mouth open and silently examined his teeth and the inside of his mouth, holding his jaw in a hard grip.

He jerked his head back and snapped his teeth at the outstretched hand.

The figure pulled back just in time and there was a sudden cessation of movement amongst all of them. The one he had tried to bite regarded him silently for a moment, then said in a dry voice, 'Subject XT743 has displayed an aggressive temperament. Whilst this may prove useful in the future, Subject XT743 must be treated with caution and disciplined when necessary. XT743, if you attempt to harm any of those who are employed for your care, you will be denied the necessary medication for your recovery and pain relief. Do you understand?'

He glared at the figure, who merely repeated the question, and then nodded. The figure registered no emotion to his hostility. Another pushed a needle into his arm, which was connected to a drip. When he asked what it was for, he was told, 'It is for essential nutrition'.

The next time they came back, they made him stand and walk, ignoring the fact that he limped and stumbled with pain and was barely able to keep himself on his feet. More than once he overbalanced and they righted him efficiently and without any compassion, ignoring any complaints or struggles.

When one hauled him by the arm, hurting him, he shouted angrily, 'It *hurts!*' His voice was still rough and his throat sore when he spoke, but it was getting easier. 'Why don't you leave me alone? It hurts, all right?!'

There was a moment's silence, then the figure said, 'The pain will pass.'

'How do you know?' he snapped.

'It always does, XT743,' it replied. 'Pain is part of the process of upgrading. Your medication already guarantees that the pain is bearable.'

'And how would you know?'

'It has been tested. The pain will pass and we will see that it does.'

'Out of the goodness of your heart?' he said sarcastically.

'No,' it responded. 'To allow you to suffer excessive pain would impair your efficiency.'

'What does that mean?'

'It means that to allow you to suffer excessive pain would impair your efficiency.'

'Why am I in any pain at all? You could give me enough pain relief to stop it hurting altogether.'

'Excessive pain relief would make you less receptive at this stage of your recovery and currently impair your responses. It is important for the XT model to be able to tolerate prescribed levels of discomfort in order to avoid impairing your efficiency in the future. It has been found that this problem is best dealt with in the early stages of recovery. The pain will pass but only when you have proven that you can tolerate the level that you are required to '

He stared at it for a moment, bewildered. 'Why?'

'It is a requirement.'

'Who from?'

'That is not your concern. You are a XT743 model. You are required to obey, not to question.'

'You just answered my questions, though,' he pointed out.

'Only in the interest of enabling you to understand your situation. Other information has not been deemed required for you to function correctly.'

'Am I allowed to ask questions?'

'You may ask. You may not receive an answer.'

'All right. Who am I?'

'You are Subject XT743.'

'But what's my name?'

'You are Subject XT743.'

'But I have a name –'

'You are Subject XT743.'

'No, I know I have a name. Everyone has a name –'

'You are Subject XT743.'

'What's your name?'

'I am YD567.'

'Do you have a name?'

'I am YD567.'

He shook his head in frustration. 'But my name –'

'You no longer have a name. You have been allocated a code.'

'Why?' he demanded.

'You have been upgraded.'

'Upgraded? What does that mean?'

'It means that you have been upgraded.'

'I don't understand –'

'It is not a requirement that you understand.'

He shook his head, frustrated. 'I won't be called that. It's not my name.'

'You are XT743. That is the only identification you require in order to function.'

'But – who was I?' he asked. 'I know I was someone –'

'Subject XT743 displays agitation due to questioning concerning a name and personal history prior to upgrade,' the figure said. 'Assistance is required. This session has been terminated. An operative will attend you shortly.'

They left.

He looked around the room. It was perhaps ten feet by ten feet, plain white with a bed and nothing else. He looked down at his hands, and noticed the scars lining every finger and across his palms and realised that these were the marks of what had been done to him. Pulling the white shirt he had been dressed in over his head, he examined the rest of his body and found so many scars that he actually felt sick and light-headed. There were scars all up his arms and legs, along his fingers and toes, and he could feel a single scar going all the way up his spine. He had none on his face, but more riddled across his chest and over his hips, circling almost every joint in his body. They were all fine, precise scars of a surgeon's blade.

He dropped his head into his hands, and wondered, *What have they done to me? What more are they going to do to me?*

It was some time before the door hissed open and a white figure appeared. 'This is Subject XT743,' it said and stepped aside, allowing another person to enter the room. It was the woman he had seen previously. She was dressed in a black skirt and jacket with a smart white shirt and high-heeled shoes. 'Thank you,' she said, and the door closed behind her, leaving them alone. She smiled up at him. 'There's no point in thanking them, because they don't appreciate it, but one finds it difficult to let go of social protocol. You are Subject XT743, yes?'

'So they tell me,' he replied shortly.

She peered over thin wire-rimmed spectacles. 'You're going to be trouble, aren't you?' she asked, sounding more amused than angry. 'The YD upgrades have informed me you have displayed aggressive behaviour and won't stop asking questions. They seem affronted, as far as they can be.' She added, 'But they were not designed to have the ability for much emotion or initiative. The XT model was designed to accommodate all of those.'

'You're not making any sense,' he said.

'I don't suppose so, no.'

'Who are you?'

'How rude of me,' she said, and held out a hand. 'I am Dr Alias. That's not my real name, obviously.' She gave a small laugh. He was obviously expected to laugh as well, and didn't.

'I thought you might have a sense of humour somewhere inside that pretty head of yours,' she said, sighing. 'Perhaps not. What did you want to know?'

27

'You're going to answer my questions?'

'You can *ask*.'

'Who am I?'

'I think you mean, who *were* you?' When he scowled, she said, 'Your name was Jonathon Mason. You were a teacher, you were mortally wounded in a recent terrorist attack and six months previously you signed a contract that, in the event of your death, your body was to be submitted for upgrade research.'

'I was injured?'

'You would have died had you not been upgraded.'

He frowned. 'I was a teacher? Called Jonathon Mason?' He shook his head. 'That doesn't feel right.'

'Of course it doesn't,' Alias said, sounding sympathetic. 'The process of upgrading tends to erase the memory. Who you were has gone, XT743. You are now a CORE upgrade.'

'A *what?*'

'A CORE upgrade. Cyber Operating Restoration Enterprise. We are a company that specialises in cyber operating systems, specifically implanting mechanical hardware into humans in order to increase life-span, cure diseases, to reduce the likelihood of injury or death. We are the cutting-edge of cyber-tech. You have been implanted with the latest in cyber-technology to replace the components of your body that were damaged beyond repair,' she said, sounding slightly impatient, 'and since you are a prototype of the XT model, your body has been mechanically strengthened, to make you stronger, less vulnerable to injury, and your reflexes have been fast-wired in order –'

'In order to what?' he demanded. 'What is an XT model,

Dr Alias? And that's a ridiculous name, by the way.'

'You don't recall the issue of upgrading?' She sounded surprised.

'Evidently not,' he said, irritated. 'So, I'm an upgrade....'

'The XT model is our newest and most sophisticated model yet '

'You're not selling me a product. Just give me the facts.'

She hesitated, as if realising for the first time that he might not be happy with what she was about to tell him. 'The XT is a security model. They are designed to function as bodyguards, security guards etc.'

'And a model of what, exactly? Some sort of robot?'

'No,' she said. 'Robotics is easy, but you try creating a robot that *truly* thinks for itself. One of our upgrades has all the human potential for emotion and initiative coupled with the strength and durability of a robot. Upgrades have, if you like, the strengths of human and machine combined with fewer of their weaknesses.'

'So that's just what you call it? An upgrade?'

'Name and description in one,' Alias said.

'And I agreed to this?'

'You *volunteered*.'

'Why would I do that?'

'You were very keen to aid us in furthering our research. Without people like you, CORE would have had a difficult time perfecting our technology.'

'But I don't remember any of this – am I ever going to regain my memory?'

'I don't know. It always depends on the individual.'

'So I'm not the same person I was before – upgrading.'

'Not exactly. Much of your personality remains the same, but the amount of memory retention differs to each upgrade. Although,' she said with a laugh, 'just from this conversation, I think you have retained a lot of your previous personality.'

'You said I'm an XT model. What are the YD models?'

'A basic servant model,' she said. 'They attend the other upgrades who have yet to be completed and contribute to the work of this facility. They have been taking care of you with a consistent efficiency that most humans are unable to manage.'

'You said they didn't have emotions.'

'Oh, they have emotions,' she said. 'Their emotions are simply more inhibited than the XT, but that was deliberate in their design.'

'Do you think that's right?' he asked. 'To have inhibited emotions?'

Her smile, which had remained stuck firmly in place until now, was beginning to slide. 'You don't understand.'

'Don't I?'

'The YD models are – were – humans that had been badly damaged, more so than you were, usually cerebral damage that meant it was difficult for us to retain memory, personality and emotion in the finished upgrade. But we don't discard them, we give them work and a purpose suited to the personality that they develop.'

'So you take the dead and turn them into – upgrades.' He sounded disgusted.

'It's more complicated than that. We don't use anyone in our research who isn't willing. Everyone who submits to upgrading has signed a contract entitling CORE to use their body for research. How they die or how badly damaged their bodies or brains are is not our fault.'

He stared at her. 'You sound awfully defensive, doctor.'

'And you know very little of what you're talking about,' Alias shot back, finally sounding angry.

He decided to back down. 'You're right, I don't. I'm just trying to understand. I'm sorry if I've offended you.' He wasn't, but she didn't know that.

'It's all right,' she said. 'You were designed to question and to make assumptions and come to intuitive conclusions. I'm only sorry that I am not able to give you complete understanding of your situation.'

'I'm just – upset that I can't recall it myself,' he said.

She nodded. 'I understand. However, it is essential that you trust me, because I can help you come to terms with your situation. You have a lot of potential, XT743, and I would hate to see that potential wasted when I have means to set your mind at rest.'

'What's going to happen to me now?'

'The process of your upgrading will be completed,' she replied. 'Then, when you have undergone testing and your upgrade has been deemed successful, you will be auctioned off.'

For a moment he stared at her with incomprehension. 'I'm sorry, did you just tell me that I'm going to be *sold* off?'

Alias nodded. 'The XT model has been promoted as the latest in security cyber-tech. You will, if you're lucky, be bought in order to act as a bodyguard or a security guard –'

'You can't do that.'

She blinked. 'Excuse me?' Her voice became suddenly

cold and authoritative. 'You don't seem to understand this situation, XT743. You are an upgrade. You have no identity outside whatever CORE decides for you. You have no freedom and no rights. I've chosen to answer your questions but I don't have to. Your demands and your ranting mean nothing to me or CORE. Your situation is simple. You have nothing that we do not choose to give you. You are dependent upon us – for *everything*.'

He stared at her. 'You can't be serious.'

'I am *deadly* serious,' she replied.

'You can't treat people like this! Like we don't have rights or freedom or choices – you can't simply do what you like and – I have a mind and free will and emotions and I have choices –'

She laughed, as if he had said something funny, but he was at a loss to think why she might be amused. 'We created you, XT743. You are our property and CORE can do what it likes with you.' She leaned forward and gently patted his cheek. 'Once your upgrade is completed and we're satisfied with the progress you have made, you'll be put up for auction and will become the property and concern of your new owner. So behave yourself and I'll see to it that you get sold to someone who'll treat you nicely and who might even give you a bit of personal freedom so you can pretend you're still a real human.'

He jerked back from her touch, shocked by the comment. 'I *am* human.'

'Not any more,' she said. 'Haven't you been paying attention? You're not a *real* human any more.'

'So you're saying I'm not a real *person* any more.'

32

'Now you're catching on,' she said approvingly. 'You're nothing more than sophisticated technology with a mind of its own. Best start getting used to it.'

'And if I don't want to?'

She laughed. 'XT743, you don't get a choice. What you want counts for nothing now. You volunteered for this, so don't turn around and complain now. We were only exercising our rights.'

'What about my rights?'

'You don't have any. Like I said, get used to it. You don't want to waste all the time and money we put into upgrading you now do you?'

'Why should I care anything for your hard work and money? What has it got me?'

'It's given you a life when you would have died,' she said.

'Maybe that would have been better!'

She gave him what was supposed to be a look of sympathy. 'A life like this is better than no life at all.'

'How would you know?' he asked softly.

Dr Alias regarded him coldly for a moment, then said, 'Make the most of the quiet time you'll have tonight,' she said. 'Tomorrow, the rest of your upgrading begins.'

'What do you mean?'

'You are one of our most sophisticated models,' she said, as if he was being particularly dense. 'The cyber-tech on the body is only part of the upgrade. The XT needs to be properly formatted and prepared for use. However,' she went on, her voice becoming colder, 'if you continue with your poor attitude and insubordination and your demands, then you will be declared a corrupt model and you will be recycled.'

33

'What does that mean?' he demanded, not wanting to show that he was afraid.

'You're a smart boy. I'm sure you can figure it out.' She patted his cheek again. 'Your world has changed. Accept it, or be recycled. That's the only choice you're going to get.' She straightened and said, 'I've wasted enough time on you, XT743. I have work to do.' She nodded to him. 'Sweet dreams – if an upgrade can dream, that is. Let me know, it'd be an interesting point for my research.' She left, the door sliding shut behind her, and a red light flashed as it was locked and he was left all alone.

Not Long Now

Lucy Delbridge

And so it began, inched its way in
Bored through my pride
To the cracks in my skin
It's mine now, it's me
And here it will be
Forever I'm servant
To one I can't see

You think I don't try
That I twist and I lie
You think I want this
That I want to die
You're wrong I want out
So I scream and I shout
I want to get better
I don't want you to doubt

I watch you watch me
I see what you see
I know that it hurts
But it's how I will be
Until it will abscond
And devour our bond

Consume through its hold
And reach through beyond

Until then I know
This is how it will go
It will gorge on me slowly
It will feed
It will grow

It will take its sweet time
It will scale
It will climb
Rise up and defeat me
With arrogant crime

Just know I'm still there
It's still me, be aware
I'm still struggling to cope
With this cross that I bare

I'm taking each day
Until it goes away
Soon I'll be free
Because I want to stay
I want to get better
I want it to let go
Each day I'm feeling
My confidence grow

It's not over yet.

The Secret of Aaah

Jan Slade

In the beginning, there was no fire in the world. The only warmth the people had was in the time of the long lights when the god Aaah rode high in the sky and the darks were short. Then it was easy to hunt, to give birth, to war against enemies, to build shelter. In the time of the long darks, these things were harder. Then the only easy things were to huddle together, or make children, or die. The god Phphp breathed on the land, and his breath was cold and covered the land in white, so even when Aaah was in the sky, there was no comfort. Sometimes Shwee would accompany Phphp and no living creature could roam in the forest. At these times, the people starved or took the animals that had stalked closer to the settlements in their own search for food. The people had learned that those killed by Phphp did not spoil as rapidly as those killed by men, but the eating was harder, as the bodies turned to stone, and flint axes were needed to chip off the flesh. The young and the old suffered much at these times as, with no teeth, they were unable to scrape the meat and take sustenance.

Life went on in this manner for many lives of men, until the people turned to the priests and said 'You are wise and magical men. Why can you not steal Aaah from the heavens so he will be with us at all times, and thereby make the hunting effortless, and make the forests blossom all the time so we may take the fruit and berries and feed our children in the time of the long darks?'

'We have tried,' said the priests, 'but we cannot get close to him. We have spoken to Aaah and asked him to stay with us so Phphp can have no power in our land, but Aaah has told us that he cannot stay with us at all times. Many are his peoples, and many are their needs, and Aaah is a loving god and must share his love among all peoples.'

Then up spake the people and said 'Then you must go to Phphp and his sister Shwee and tell them they are not welcome in this land and they must follow Aaah and visit the other peoples with him.' However, the priests told them that it was the way of the gods that Aaah could not live high in the heavens at the same time as Phphp was in the world. Therefore, the people turned against their priests and told them that they must use their powers to find a way through the long darks. If they failed then the people would kill them and put their bodies to better use. Men waved their spears and smacked their lips when saying this and when the priests saw this they were sore afraid, for, being wise men, they knew the meaning behind the action.

The priests left the settlement and, calling others of their kind, they gathered at the holy place to consider the problem, but even after many light times they found no solution.

Then up spake Pheelor, son of Dron, the chief priest, and he said, 'I know a way to steal a piece of Aaah and keep him with us in the time of the long darks.'

At first, the priests would not allow him to speak. 'He is a young man and not yet a priest,' they said, but Dron said that soon Pheelor would undergo the mysteries and should have his say. 'He is yet young, as you say, but we, in our age and wisdom, have been unable to find the answer. Perhaps this boy will be a better priest than any of us and already has the gift of knowledge. Let him speak.' And such was the power of Dron, that all present dropped their objections.

So Pheelor rose to his feet and spake thus: 'I have noticed when water falls from the heavens and the god Buroondurw rages around the skies, shouting his war cry, Aaah is angry and throws his spears to strike his enemy down, but Buroondurw is wily and many spears fall to the earth. I will go into the forest and I will catch one of these weapons and we will have a part of Aaah with us at all times.'

The wise men exclaimed at this and Dron said, 'No, my son, that is the way to certain death. You shall not go.' But the wise men, who were jealous of Dron, and did not want his son to succeed him, over-ruled his words.

'If the boy thinks he can do it then he must try,' they said. 'The future of our people depends upon it.'

Dron bowed his head and, with a heavy heart, gave his consent.

At this, the other priests saw their opportunity and decreed that Pheelor was forbidden, on pain of death, to return to the settlement until his task was completed.

When next the water fell from the heavens and Buroondurw voiced his anger Pheelor went into the forest and tried to capture a spear of Aaah, but he was never able to get near enough. He followed Buroondurw for many hunting distances, resting when the god rested and resuming the hunt when Buroondurw again ranged the heavens. At last, weary, and sure his quest was doomed, Pheelor lay on the forest floor and awaited death. Even when Buroondurw called to him, he was too exhausted to move. The battle raged around him and Aaah sent many spears, which hit the earth and nearby trees, but Pheelor had no strength left. When the gods ceased their warring, Pheelor slept.

When he awoke the forest was still, and Aaah was in the sky, gently giving his warmth to the world. As Pheelor gazed around, he suddenly knew his hunt was over.

He made his way back to the settlement as fast as he could, but when the people saw him they were angry that he carried none of Aaah's spears.

'Why have you returned?' they cried. 'You have brought us nothing and now must die.'

Pheelor raised his hands and said, 'Wait, I must talk to my father and the other priests. You see nothing in my hands, but I have indeed brought Aaah's warmth with me. Now we shall never have to suffer again during the long darks; but this is a holy matter and I will only show the priests.'

So priests were summoned and when all were gathered they took Pheelor to the holy place and Dron said unto him

'You have returned, my son, but where is the spear of Aaah you say you carry?'

Pheelor took some sticks from his garments and showed them to the priests.

'When I was at the end of my strength, and could journey no longer, Buroondurw and Aaah had a great battle. When it ended I fell into a deep sleep, but Aaah came to me in his victory and showed me the way to keep him with us.'

So saying, he knelt down and began to rub the sticks together. Faster and faster he rubbed until a faint wisp of smoke, and then a small flame came from the sticks. Soon the priests began to push smaller twigs and dried grasses onto the flame until the small mound was burning brightly.

Then Dron asked, 'How do you know this, my son?'

'While I travelled through the forest I saw that many of Aaah's spears hit the trees, and I saw that Aaah had put his warmth in the wood. Aaah showed me how to get it out in my dream.'

When the priests heard this, they threw themselves at Pheelor's feet and said, 'You are truly a great priest, and beloved of Aaah,' and there was no more talk of his death.

So ended the tyranny of Phphp and Shwee over the land in the long dark, and so the people prospered and multiplied.

*

NB. This legend is taken from the treatise written by O.R.Eally, History Professor Emeritus, UCM, entitled 'Homo Sapiens; The Early Years'. This in itself is a prequel to his earlier work, 'Homo Sapiens; An Upright People'.

Professor Eally notes in his chapter 'Post Neanderthal

Period; Nature or Nurture' that 'Language was in a state of flux at this time and many things were named after the noise they made, or the sound a man would make when seeing the object. Hence the animal we now know as a lion was then called an "Aaargh", this being the last sound made by a man who had unexpectedly met one in the forest. Of course, pronunciation was of great importance so no confusion could arise if a man said "Aaah has come," "Aaah" being the sound a man made when he felt the warmth of the sun on his face.'

The word Phphp (the sound of snow falling) is another case in point. It is essential to enunciate the final 'p' so as to distinguish it from a commonly used expletive, as in: 'Oh, Phph...'

By following these rules the names of other gods will be self-explanatory.

BEING

Friday Night

Llinos Jones

We swap partners on the dancefloor,
Yours is too thin for you
Mine too short for me
And both are amenable and laugh as we
                                    sidestep
To site our new targets.
The lights swirl, rainbowed and dazzling
Flashing his skin with vibrancy
As our bodies thud to the throb of the beat.
A secret machine frees dry ice behind the DJ
To tumble through the throngs
Of strutting youth, this teenage swagger.
It gathers around our feet, pools and plumps
In flaring gaudy hues, a numinous mist
As our eyes lock in this lavish twilight.
We retreat to darkened alcoves,
Shout whispers through shadows
Until we reach out.

Eleven o'clock and fluorescent lights flash
A pub, awash with smoke and acrid scent
Emerges. His face, still endearing, is
                        harshly lit
But his skin is coarse and scarred. We
                   unlock our limbs,
Smile in self-conscious smugness
And part.

On the bus home, giggling and woozy with
my friends
I realize.
I don't know his name.

You Won't Even Notice I'm Here

A Monologue

Katy Griffiths

Hello, is this seat taken? Oh, sorry, you're waiting for your friend. Well, I'll just pop myself down until she gets here. If you don't mind, of course. I don't want to be forcing myself on people; that would be very rude. You don't have to worry; you won't even notice I'm here. I'll be ever so quiet, like a little church mouse, I am. I'll be come and gone in an instant, like a dream. You'll wake up tomorrow and wonder if I ever existed, that's how quiet I can be, you see! My mother always says she's surprised to see me sitting in the corner of the kitchen, as she never notices when I arrive. Too busy gossiping to one of her friends, I expect, on the phone. She's on that bloody phone night and day. Honestly, some people have no consideration.

You're new round here, aren't you? Yes, I thought I hadn't seen you before; never forget a face, especially one as...

noticeable as yours. Not so good with names, mind you. Oh no! I wasn't suggesting there was anything wrong with your face at all love, no, no, no; I would never be so insensitive. My mother always says I'm far too sensitive, sensitive is my middle name. Well, actually it's Patricia, but you get the idea. It's alright love, I was only joking. My name's Angela, by the way. And you are... Maria, well isn't that a lovely name. Neighbour of ours had a poodle by that name. Lovely animal, but used to leave terrible skid marks on the sheepskin rug. You'd think it wouldn't hurt to give the dog a wash once in a while. Mind you, she was stinking herself, so the poor old dog had no chance. It could turn nasty, mind you. The moment her back was turned, that dog launched at me like a thing possessed. It was like part poodle, part rottweiler. I don't go around there any more, it's too traumatic. Not that it's much of a loss. She used to serve terrible biscuits.

How old are you then dear? Twenty four! Have you got a boyfriend yet then? No! Well, I don't know what's wrong with young men today. I mean, it's not as if you're that repulsive. If you just had a pick at those spots, you'd be quite presentable. Oh now, don't upset yourself love, I'm sure they'll pop out in time. It's just your hormones; they go straight to the face in some people. Here, dry your eyes love, people are staring. It's alright, she's a bit emotional. Boyfriend trouble. She hasn't got one. Oh, fine then, bugger off. I was only trying to help. Honestly, young people today. Got no manners, some of them.

Hello, do you mind if I just park myself down by here. You're waiting for your sister, are you? Oh, well you just tell me, as soon as you see her, and then I'll be on my way. I just have to sit down, I'm afraid dear; it's my knees you see. Ahhh, isn't he a pretty baby. Oh, it's a she, I'm ever so sorry. Lovely nose on her; very shapely. My father had a nose just like that, after he fell off that ladder. Said it used to add character. He only went up to clear the guttering. Terrible thing it was; he was in agony of pain for hours. And he completely ruined my ladder. I wouldn't mind, but I'd only just bought it, so that was just money down the drain. I did contact the manufacturer, but they said it was less to do with the ladder, and more to do with the person who fell off it. Disgraceful behaviour, if you want my opinion. So, I suggest you keep this little one away from ladders, dear little soul. Mind you, in her case, it might make an improvement. Cheaper than plastic surgery any day, dear. Oh, well fine, be like that. Huffy little madam, I was only joking. Can't anybody take a joke these days? Some people are so sensitive.

Good afternoon, lovely day isn't it? You wouldn't mind if I just perched myself on this stool, would you dear. I'm desperate for a cuppa. Your friend will be here in just a minute, oh well that's fine, as soon as she gets here, I'll just buzz off. Don't want to be a nuisance to anybody. You don't know if they serve any biscuits around here, do you? No, shame that, I could just fancy a Bourbon. That's the biscuit love, not the drink. Don't want you thinking I'm an alcoholic. I mean I like a drink, but I can always control it, see. I think that's the key to a healthy lifestyle. But then you look skinny enough, I don't need to tell you that.

Not anorexic are you love? You look like you could do

with a solid meal. It won't do you any good you know dear, men can't stand hugging skin and bones. You're not, oh good. I hate to see these girls walking around like bloody pencils. Got heads like lollipops, it's not right. My friend Mavis went like that once, like a bloody stick she was. I went round to see her, and you could have lost her in her own armchair. Terrible thing, dieting; although if you ask me it was pure laziness. Couldn't be bothered to cook, so she lived on Complan for six months. Dreadful that stuff, full of vitamins and minerals, but tastes like shit. I told her, she'd have been better off on dog food. I'd cook for her myself, but I can't walk that far, see love, not with my hips. And the miserable bugger never let's you in when you do call. Some people are so rude. I mean, there must be some reason she doesn't want me in there. I've never had so much as a glimpse at her new cottage suite.

Are you sure you're not anorexic dear, you're making very heavy weather of that muffin? If you spew it back up, you'll waste your money. Better spent in your stomach than a toilet bowl, dear, and you don't look like you've got much to spare, by the state of those clothes. Oh, you can see your friend over there, can you? Alright love, tata then.

Funny girl she was. Hardly said a word to me. So rude. My mother always says that rudeness is the most terrible thing.... Oh hello. I don't think I've seen you around here before, have I? My name's Angela, pleased to meet you too dear. You're waiting for your husband, are you love? Well, don't mind me dear, you won't even notice I'm here. So, you've got a husband, have you, dear? Any babies yet?

Grandpa

Penny Sutton

Why Grandpa is it just for her you smile?
Her little quirks make you guffaw, she's cute.
She's too young to know the meaning of guile.

You glare at me, your ice blue eyes pierce while
your threepenny moneybox she will loot.
Why Grandpa is it just for her you smile?

Her asks you never ignore, but I rile.
It's only me you ever tell to scoot.
She's too young to know the meaning of guile.

She's being entertained – it's me in exile.
TV requests? For her you always root.
Why Grandpa is it just for her you smile?

She's not scared of you, just thoughtless. She's vile.
Never sees the undone lace on your boot.
She's too young to know the meaning of guile.

Compassion and patience is not her style.
Centre of attention, selfish to suit.
Why Grandpa is it just for her you smile?
She's too young to know the meaning of guile.

Bloody Thorns

Sarah Tanner

There were roses with crimson petals the colour of blood, the scent intoxicating and seductive. There were roses in the grey wilderness of the crumbling ruins of a once magnificent castle. There were roses with thorns like swords that would slice through flesh and draw blood that stained the stone and perfectly matched the hue of the flowers.

This was the sleeping castle, under a spell for a hundred years, and the time had come for it to be broken.

The prince came, as had been foretold a century before. He was young and he was handsome with eyes the colour of rain clouds and hair the colour of salt. He rode a white charger and wore silver armour and carried a ruby-hilted sword.

He had been born and raised to this destiny, to break the spell, to rescue the princess and in doing so gain love easily and eternally. For this he had left his home, journeyed far and wide and come to the sleeping castle, sword in hand to battle the guarding thorns that had torn many suitors before him to pieces and given the roses their blazing colour.

The palace had decayed in the one hundred years that had passed, the roses had taken over and the spiders had also invaded, weaving shrouds amidst the dust of a century. The sleeping castle lay quiet and undisturbed, inhabited only by those who lay in slumber, a single breath from death.

The thorns did not part the way for him.

He fought them savagely, hacking at them with his sword, beheading blooms and scattering their petals in sinister snowfalls.

Those in his way did not submit to their execution without a fight of their own. For every blow he landed upon them the thorns returned another, ripping and tearing through flesh, drawing blood with edges as sharp as any blade.

The prince continued and cut his way through the roses, leaving a crimson path of fallen petals behind him, the colour of his blood indistinguishable from the colour of the flowers.

He made his way to the highest room of the tallest tower, exhausted and covered in sweat and blood, every inch the battle-scarred hero.

Love and fate make fools of all.

Even this room had not escaped the ravages of one hundred years. The briers and the spiders had had their way here too. There was not an inch of floor or wall that was not touched by webs or flowers, now crushed beneath the prince's feet, the webs and dust sent swirling into the stale air by his presence.

The spinning wheel lay shattered on the floor, the needle still stained an ugly red.

And there she was, lying asleep, beneath a blanket of roses.

He cast them aside.

There she was. Buried beneath a shroud of roses lay the desiccated remains of the sleeping beauty, as decayed as the castle around her. Not even she had escaped the passing of one hundred years. Not even in enchanted sleep.

Yet, as he gazed down at her, he saw that life still lingered. So soft that he almost didn't notice it, a breath escaped from between her dried lips. Life still lingered and, as aged as she was, she could still be awakened by that one kiss.

He had come to awaken the sleeping beauty and though no longer a beauty still she slept. He had come to awaken her, had spent his life preparing to awaken the sleeping beauty.

One kiss was all it took.

She sighed, the whisper of the wind through a dead tree's branches, and opened her eyes.

For a moment yellowed and ancient eyes that were almost blinded with age met clear grey eyes and understood the gulf of one hundred years between them.

She drew in a single breath that rattled like broken bones, and smiled.

Then her eyes closed and her breath faded into nothingness.

The sleeping beauty slept no more.

And the prince stood in the silent tower with his blood staining the stone floor while around him the roses withered and died.

Crimson Snow

Caroline James

Run, running fast on crunchy snow
In the distance, gaining pace, moving in
Smelling odour, sniffing tracks,
Panting, snorting deep tread.

Glistening snow, blue black hush of dusk
Stillness, ears pricked heightened
Eyes darting, bulging, rippling pelt
Move on cover of darkness.

Shadows, watch, listen, burrow undergrowth
Shuffling, danger, poised crouched
White breath rising, on ice clouds
Retreat to seek, find, wean.

Scurry, hide hole onto open ground
Silent, graceful, cutting into air
Prancing, jumping, gliding
Into arms of death

Whirring, echoing, spitting through
Dusky cloud, velocity, thud, numbness
Black cordite, white death, eyes bright
Bulged on crimson snow

Snow covered mound, hidden, buried
Waiting to be suckled
No light, needful, barely born
Eyes glued; extinction.

Duty Free

Penny Sutton

Fiona slid out of her shorts and skimpy top and wrapped her pale blue kikoyi around her and stood at the door of the rondavel. The tide was out and miles of white beach sparkled under the midday African sun. Only a couple of brave, or foolish, tourists walked among the coral pools. With her blonde hair and fair skin she was well aware of the dangers of the midday sun. It would be no sunbathing for her, her spray tan ensured she didn't stand out as a gullible tourist.

Mark wasn't tall, dark or handsome, in fact he was quite short, a bit stocky and with a mop of unruly brown curly hair which could have been tidied up with a good haircut; now she was sounding like her mother! But his eyes were electric. Pools of green quartz were framed with the longest lashes she had ever seen on a man. A chance meeting at the police station where she worked, something to do with nosy neighbours she remembered, led to one date then another, and another....

There had been a lot of envy, and banter, at work when Mark had asked her to go on holiday with him. 'You've not even done the meeting parents bit yet,' Rachel had chided.

'Yeah, I know. But there isn't time if we're to miss the rains, Mark says.'

The prospect of visiting somewhere she had only ever heard her grandfather talking about, recounting his bachelor days in the District Commissioner's office at Voi and the glorious beaches on the coast, overruled her natural and professional caution. 'It's only a holiday. It's not as if I'm marrying the guy,' she had joked.

'You go and enjoy yourself, lass,' Chris, her boss, chipped in, 'but just be careful.'

*

Mark hadn't mentioned the primitive accommodation, he may have suspected her disapproval! All he said was that it would be idyllic. It was. Quaint whitewashed mud walls, two wooden shutters with internal mesh fly screens opening to a view of the sea, a conical thatch roof insulating the inside from the heat, and the cold in the African winter, Mark had explained. She tried not to think of the local inhabitants in the roof space; fortunately the mosquito net enveloping the bed allowed her to sleep without worrying too much about unwanted intruders.

'And we can go walking on the beach, swimming, water skiing and scuba diving,' Mark had chattered on. 'You'll love scuba diving! The fish, the coral, the colours...'

'You'll not get me.... No. No. No.' She could feel her voice getting louder, almost hysterical.

'What's up babe?' Mark moved towards her, put his arm round her shoulder.

Fiona pulled away, she didn't want him to see her tears. She thought she had put that childhood disaster to the back of her mind but those awful memories of her stepfather and his 'secret games' in the bath came flooding back. She could feel the blood rushing to her head, water rushing into her ears, splashing on her face. She felt quite faint.

'C'mon Fi, just think what...'

'Don't call me that. And... leave me, leave me alone. Just go.' Fiona gathered what strength she had and walked away. She stooped to pick up a stick and began doodling in the sand before sitting herself against a palm tree. She could see Mark from the corner of her eye, staring at her with a totally bemused expression on his face. Fiona looked up at him. 'Mark.'

He smiled, still with a hurt look on his face.

'Mark, it's not you. It's just... oh, nothing.'

Mark came and sat down beside her. He took her hand and caressed it. 'I'm sorry.' He waited, obviously wanting her to say something.

She smiled, fighting back tears. 'I just don't want to talk about it. You go, I'll be fine here.'

He lifted her hand up, stroked it tenderly before kissing it. 'Fancy some lunch?'

*

Lunch was jumbo prawns in a delicious local spicy sauce, washed down with ice cold Pinot Grigio and fresh mangoes for desert. Mark was right, everything did taste so fresh or was it because she had time to savour each mouthful? She had seen the local fisherman delivering their catch each day and fruit dripped from the surrounding trees. The place really was magical.

She felt quite light headed and was going to relax with her book. Mark was not a reader and had made derogatory comments about her choice of book for the trip. She couldn't admit it wasn't her normal sort of book, but the title had grabbed her as she flew into the bookshop at the airport, steering well clear of the sob-story childhoods which seemed to dominate most of the shelf space. This was so exciting, a thriller about the smugglers in Victorian times, using the sewers to conceal their booty.

Sinking on to the bed and closing her eyes, she tried to forget the incident before lunch. She had half hoped he would have cancelled his diving trip, but maybe they would have a walk along the beach later this evening. She would have to find some more reading matter if this was to be the pattern for the whole holiday. She looked up to the roof, and turned away quickly, not wanting to see any creepy crawlies! She hoped they slept during the day. The palm trees were dancing in the breeze, the rustle creating an opera all of its own. She could see the beach from where she was. Maybe they would go for a swim later when the tide was in, if he hadn't had enough of the sea for one day.

She opened her book and was soon submerged in the underworld. Echoes of an impending storm bounced off the ancient brickwork, torchlight beamed through the sewer, glancing off damp walls, and died in empty crannies. Rats scampered everywhere, darting through channels, along ledges, over feet. She shivered.

*

Crack. The book crashed on to her nose. Lifting it she saw it was getting dark and she could hear the wind roaring. The sky lit up and then crack – more thunder. She saw forks of lightning cut through the sky and light up the foaming tide. This was very different from the rumbling thunder and odd bit of sheet lightning they occasionally got on the east coast of England.

She felt on the bedside table for the matches to light the candles. There was a breeze coming through the windows which made this difficult. As soon as she got a small flame going, she put the glass cover over it. The glimmer grew gradually and lit the room up, the shadows were playing hide-and-seek. It would be better to close the windows. Gingerly opening the door, she was met by a rush of warm, damp air. She crept round the rondavel, in the shelter of the roof, unhooked the shutters and pushed them closed. She would need to latch them shut from the inside. She went back in to secure them.

The storm was like a magnet and she found herself opening the door and looking out. She stared in amazement, this was a storm like no other she had ever seen, but it was still warm. She watched a commotion on the shore, powerful lights arcing this way and that; at times she could see the light shining through shards of rain and, for a moment, forgot about the people, forgot about the dangers they and she could be facing with the lightning all around.

Once the storm calmed it was black, an eerie black. Fiona felt goose bumps along her arms. With just her kikoyi around her she decided to put more clothes on. She went back into the rondavel and closed the door. The flickering candle light brought images to her mind, images of pirates making their way along tunnels to stash away their looted cargoes. Maybe they were pirates on the beach tonight? What was in the caves on the headland? They had walked past there on several occasions, but never ventured further than the sandy entrance. What if... her mind was jumping around. Where was Mark? Was he safe?

She reached for her mobile to see what the time was. A quarter past seven. 'He's usually back before dark.' As she put the phone on the table it beeped, she opened it, the dial lit up – 1 message received. In Ngongwe Bar 4 beer, back soon. M.

She looked at the text again and replied: ok, c u soon. Well this was going to be an exciting evening she thought to herself, and decided to go back to her book while she waited for him.

Propping the pillows up on the bed she settled herself down to read. The candles flickered around the small room as she released the mosquito net. It wasn't long before she was engrossed once again.

Getting up for the call of nature she realised the rain had stopped, although the wind was still whistling through the eaves. She looked at her mobile: it was now half past nine and still no Mark. Not wanting to sound like the proverbial nagging wife she decided not to text, but sit and wait patiently, even if she was becoming mildly irritated by the whole affair.

No, she would go for a walk. Gathering a torch and her mobile she opened the door and went out towards the beach. The tide was in and waves crashed on to the sand in huge breakers, the palm trees looked like long legged ballet dancers, their tutus gyrating in tune to the roar of the tide and the rustling leaves. Fanning the torch light out in front of her as she went, she caught the glinting light pools of water in dead banana leaves. There was no one around, the solitude felt strange. There had always been someone on the beach.

Fiona clasped her mobile to her chest, waiting for it to throb a call. Surely Mark would at least text her? There was no one close by she could call on, she would have to wait patiently. She walked on towards the headland, kicking up the loose sand as she went. It was the last place she had seen any sign of life, but there were no arc lights now in the dark sky. Where the tide had been it was flat, like a newly made bed, and a few brave crabs were darting about. Her footsteps were sinking into the soft sand on the foreshore; grains gathered across the soles of her flip flops and flew out as she took each step. It was something for her to concentrate on, take her mind off the unanswered questions racing through her mind.

As she neared the caves she noticed an upturned boat, the only sign that anyone had ever been here. She walked closer to it. The sand was trampled around it, tufts of grass were bent over. She kicked at one tuft and something flew out, it glinted in her torch light. She knelt to see what it was. A medallion. Picking it up she turned it over, a St, Christopher just like the one Mark always wore. He said he needed luck in his journeys. Maybe the owner had been lucky, rescued from the jaws of the earlier storm. She picked it up and put it safely in her pocket, hoping she would find the owner so she could return it.

She walked further inland. There were deep rutted tyre marks, it looked as if a vehicle had swung in at speed as the ruts formed an almost perfect circle. Her mobile vibrated in her hand, she didn't recognise the number, but before she could answer it, it rang off. She called the number back but it went straight into voice mail and, unsure who it was, she decided not to leave a message. She put the mobile into her pocket and headed back to the rondavel.

The trees were now still. She thought she heard a rustling in the undergrowth behind the boat but when she trained her torch towards the noise everything was silent. She began to walk on again, quickening her step. She wanted to be in the security of the rondavel. As she neared the chalet her mobile vibrated in her pocket again. She jumped even though she was expecting it. It had to be Mark. 1 message received. Fumbling to open it, she felt her heart beat faster. This was turning into a nightmare: 'RU OK?' But it wasn't from Mark's phone.

It was her boss, Chris. Snapping her mobile shut, 'What's that got to do with you?' she shouted to anyone who would listen. 'I am on leave... and will be for the next ten days.'

Her inquisitive police mind kicked in, she would have to

reply. Opening the phone, she stumblingly managed to reply: 'Not really.' She barely had time to put the phone down when it beeped a reply: 'Is Mark with you?'

'No, why?' flew back.

She began pacing the room, her mind full of the day's events. Her train of thought was interrupted by another message on the mobile. This must be Mark. 'RU alone?' Chris again. She was now beginning to feel irritated and replied curtly 'Yes' and before she had time to exit the menu, her phone rang. She jumped as she answered it. It was Chris, still not Mark.

'Hi Chris,' she managed to answer coolly, trying to hide her impatience.

'Fiona, there's a problem.' Chris's voice was calm, professional. She felt like a suspect being interrogated. 'Fiona, it's about Mark.'

'Where is he?' she was quick to ask.

'Fiona, sit down. What do you know about him?'

'What do you mean. He's a guy and pretty unreliable at that. Nothing new there...'

'Fiona, Fiona, don't be flippant. There is a problem.'

'Oh yes.'

'Fiona where are you?'

'In the rondavel, why?'

'Do you have your passports handy? Yours and Mark's?'

'I presume so, why?'

'Look, can you just give me straight answers, this is serious.'

Fiona went to the top drawer of the dressing table. It was locked and she had no idea where the key was. She looked around the room, her eyes settled on Mark's bedside table. Fingering through papers, there was a Playboy magazine, some paracetamol, tissues, but no key.

'Er... Chris, there is a locked drawer, but no key.'

'Fiona, I don't think Mark is who you think he is.'

'What d'you mean?' Fiona's legs began to tremble. The candles were flickering their last breath of life. She went to the chair by the door and grabbed the torch. Her instinct was to run. Run anywhere. But where. Without her passport she wouldn't get far.

'Oh my god, Chris... Chris are you still there?'

'Yes, I'm on the other line to the Chief of Police in Mombasa. He says he wants to take you in for interrogation. He thinks you're part of a scam.'

'No, no, Chris. What scam, what's happening?' In her agitated state, everything seemed surreal.

'Fiona, do you know where you are?'

'Not really. Mark drove. We came over a bridge. I think he said the Ocean View Hotel was a little further up the road, but I haven't been there, so I don't know. There is no one around here. And it's close to midnight.'

'Fiona, you can't stay there. You've got to go somewhere. They'll know where to find you and I can't risk them taking you. You know what these places are like.' There was a long pause. 'We need you here.'

Fiona clutched the torch to her chest. She heard the rev of vehicle engines, fragmented shards of light shone through the shutters.

'Chris, they're coming.'

'For god's sake Fiona hide, don't run out now, they'll get

you. Just keep this line open. I won't speak, I need to know what's going on.'

'OK.'

Fiona moved the cases from under the bed and slid as far back as she could, pulling the cases in behind her.

There was a knock on the door. She froze and took a slow silent breath. She heard muffled speaking, but couldn't make out any words. It might be Mark, he spoke Swahili. She would wait until he identified himself. Even then, with what she now suspected, she wasn't sure she wanted to see him again.

There was a louder bang on the door and more high pitched speaking, 'Miss Grant, Miss Grant are you there. We need to speak with you.'

Fiona chilled at the sound of her name and lay completely still, hoping Chris could hear what was going on. She turned the microphone of her phone towards the sound.

There was another bang on the door, this time louder and more agitated.

A crack and the door flew open. A rush of warm air flowed in, carrying a distinct smell of hot sweaty bodies. The chatter was louder, now obviously in the room. Fiona could see torch beams flashing, she presumed they were scanning the room. She could hear footsteps coming closer. A beam of light seeped above the suitcase. Curling up, she clutched the phone to her chest. Stopped breathing. She could hear drawers being opened and closed. The bathroom door squeaked open. Whoever it was – they were – had stopped speaking. No doubt they were now listening. Listening for the sound of her heartbeat?

Fiona closed her eyes and recalled a child protection raid she had done with Chris when they found a child in a cupboard. Her last case? She hoped and prayed these people wouldn't find her.

The footsteps stopped, one voice spoke, in a calm tone, another language. The light dimmed. Maybe they were going? She hoped. She waited. Wanted to hear the vehicle moving away, but silence. 'If they were any good at their job,' she thought, 'they would now be scouring outside.' Not that that would be difficult, as it was a wide open space, dotted with the odd palm tree. The undergrowth was a good couple of hundred yards away.

Fiona whispered into the phone. 'Chris, you still there?'

'Yes, well done. Just stay where you are. They may have left someone on guard. Don't hang up. We're getting a GPS of your position.'

'OK, thanks.'

Fiona lay still, straining to hear any noise.

After what seemed like hours she heard voices again. They were coming closer. Car doors slammed, an engine spluttered into life, revved up and then grew fainter.

'I think they've gone,' she whispered into the phone.

'Good.'

'I'm going to get out and look around.'

'Don't you take any unnecessary risks.' A bit late for that she thought.

'OK, OK.'

Fiona slowly slid the suitcase out in front of her and crawled out. She stopped. Waited. Listened. No voices, just the gentle rustling of the trees outside and the sea in the distance. They had left the door open. Walking to the doorway she ventured on to the step, but couldn't see anything. The beach was still deserted. The sky was a dark grey, dawn was not far away.

Returning to the rondavel, she intended to pack up her things. She wanted to get out of here. She would make her way up the beach and see if she could find the hotel. But she needed her passport.

Fiona was inspecting the locked drawer, when she heard a faint 'Fi... o... na' from somewhere. She turned round and saw in the doorway an apparition with torn clothes and covered in blood.

'Fiona, it's me, Mark.'

'Bloody hell. Where've you been?' Her anger subsided when she realised he needed urgent help. She should have taken off, but something inside her told her to get him cleaned up. Perhaps it was the 'human rights' issue which had been drummed into them in the force, or maybe it was....

'What's your case doing there? You're not leaving, are you? Fiona, you can't leave me,' his pathetic voice stammered.

'Oh, I was just looking to see if I had another book,' she lied and then sarcastically spat out, 'I've finished the one I bought at Heathrow.'

'Oh,' was all he muttered in reply.

She went back to him, helped him on to the bathroom chair and began removing the disgusting clothes and cleaning up the wounds beneath.

'Mark, you should see a doctor. Where is the car?'

'It's by the diving shop. You can't take me anywhere. They'll get us both.'

'What are you talking about?'

Fiona looked into Mark's face, his eyes glazed and a sad effort at a grin appeared.

'Come on, I think the shower will be the best place for you.'

She couldn't think where any compassion was coming from.

'Didn't you wear your St Christopher today?' she asked calmly.

'Er, no. I must have left it beside my bed.'

Fiona decided to say nothing about her find. After all the initials, CMD, weren't his anyway. But then who was he?

Once the blood was washed away Mark looked more human. Keeping the conversation light Fiona remarked 'Hey, these bruises are corkers, any more and your passport would look like a fake!'

'How d'you know?'

'Well I didn't recognise you when you walked in.'

'Oh.'

'You'd better tell me what happened.'

'It's best you don't know.'

'I don't think so. You brought me all the way out here, left me all night in a dreadful storm, didn't bother to call. I think you owe it to me. What have I walked into?'

'Oh, just an argument when we were diving.'

'Oh yes. What about?'

'There's a wreck off the coast, it's good diving around there. The fish swimming in the broken...'

'Yeah, yeah. Cut out the crap. What really happened?'

'There were these chaps, they were nicking the brass and

stuff from the sunken boat.'

'Yes, and?'

'Well it sort of erupted and when we got ashore there was a punch up.'

'So what about the text from the... whatever the bar was?'

'What text?'

'So you didn't even bother to try and contact me?'

'I couldn't. I couldn't find my phone.'

'That's pathetic, you expect me to believe that.'

'Fi... ona, it's true. Honestly.'

'I'm not green. It might have escaped your mind that I'm a police officer. I've seen punch ups on a Saturday night outside the pub. The odd bloody face, yeah, but you look like you've been mauled by a herd of elephant.'

'You don't understand. They're really vicious here... and primitive.'

'Yeah, yeah.'

Fiona's mobile beeped, Mark jumped. 'Oh god. Who's that?' He was on his feet and heading for the door.

'It's work, they want some info.'

Grabbing the first clothes he could find, he put them on quickly. 'I can't stick around here.' Hobbling to the door, he steadied himself before launching his battered body off in the direction of the undergrowth. Fiona stood watching, intrigued. 'Was that commotion last night anything to do with him?' she asked herself. Feeling her mobile vibrating in her pocket she took it out. help on its way chris.

When she looked back Mark had been joined by three, or was it four people, voices shouting, arms flailing. There was a clash of metal on metal. Duty said she should intervene, Fiona said 'I don't think so.' Turning round to go back into the rondavel she saw a vehicle heading for her. Her heart leapt. Was this Chris's help?

A tall man dressed in a light safari suit leapt out. He had a moustache and wore sun glasses; she wanted to see his eyes, she wanted to know who she was dealing with. He strode towards her with an outstretched hand, and, removing his glasses with the other hand, introduced himself.

'Hi, I'm Dave Ennis, I'm from the British Consulate. Chris has sent me.'

'Thank god for that.' Fiona pointed in Mark's direction, the fracas had become more frantic. Ennis took Fiona's forearm.

'Don't go. The authorities know about him. The police are on their way.'

'Get me out of here, quick.' Fiona freed herself from his grasp and darted back into the rondavel.

'They're looking for me too. Chris said.'

Ennis took three long strides and put his hand on her shoulder, 'It's OK, a lot has been going on in the background. We need to be here when the police arrive.'

Fiona's hands became clammy, she pulled away from him, threw her case open and began flinging things into it. 'Can you get the drawer open?' she yelled at Ennis. 'My passport's in there.'

'Yes. Yes, I know about that.' He produced an array of small screwdrivers from his pocket and began to fiddle with the lock. The drawer opened and there on the top was her passport and one for Craig Mark Daniels. Ennis opened it and, showing the photo to her, asked, 'Is this him?'

'Yes, he told me he was Mark Hawkins.'

'Well now you know.'

Fiona felt in her pocket for the medallion and pulled it out. 'That's what the initials CMD are for, I assume.'

'Where did you get that?'

'I found this last night by the upturned boat,' pointing towards the melee.

'Interesting.'

'Yes, I asked him where his medallion was and he said it was on his bedside table.'

'So he's been back has he?'

'God, he crawled in here looking as if he had been in a ruck with wild life. I did manage to get him into the shower. But as soon as my phone beeped, he was off like a bullet. Into the jaws of the lion's den by the looks of things.' Fiona gesticulated towards the group.

Turning back, she shut her case. Ennis picked it up and as they were walking towards his car they saw the police arrive.

They drove straight towards the undergrowth, and then veered towards the upturned boat.

'We'll just wait here. They'll come over, when they're ready.'

Fiona and Ennis watched as the police surrounded the bush. Police dogs were barking, darting in and out of the undergrowth. Bodies were being handcuffed and bundled into the vehicle. A lone policeman strode towards them.

He greeted Ennis with 'Bwana, asante,' and smiled.

He turned towards Fiona and offered his hand, bowing

his head, 'Thank you madam, you have been most helpful.'

Fiona glanced at Ennis, her look asked if she should divulge the whereabouts of Mark's medallion. Ennis answered for her.

'Oh Peter, have you got an exhibit pouch with you? Miss Grant found this last night and recognised it. She had no idea he was here last night.'

'Oh yes, I will get one from the van.'

Once he was out of earshot Ennis looked at Fiona, 'And they'll probably want the passport we've just found too.'

On his return he approached Fiona. 'Miss Grant, we might need you to give evidence for us. I have spoken to Bwana Chris and he is happy for you to be released for that.'

Fiona felt a dull ache in the pit of her stomach, realising just how close she had come to being dragged into whatever this was.

Ennis opened the car door for her. She got in, grateful to sit down.

*

'What if they'd come to the rondavel to find him?' she spoke her thoughts aloud.

'Hmm. Yes. That's what we were afraid of.'

Fiona's skin went quite cold, it twitched, as if there were rats crawling all over it. She began to shiver, shake. Felt hot. And cold. Ennis looked over towards her.

'Are you alright?'

'I don't know.'

He turned off the road, the signpost was for Ocean View Hotel.

'We'll stop here for a cup of something warm for you. Get yourself something warm to wear. You're in shock.'

They walked into the hotel, Dave went up to a waiter and spoke in another language. Fiona looked on, her mind was glazing in and out of reality. They went to sit down in a warm corner of the lounge. No sooner had they sat down than a tray of tea appeared, with a plate of chocolate biscuits.

Fiona clasped her hands round the teacup and sipped slowly. Warmth gradually crept back into her body. She relaxed and looked at Ennis. He was obviously waiting for her to speak.

'What's going on?'

'Don't you know?'

'No. All Mark, or perhaps I should say Craig, said was that he got into a fight because some locals were plundering a wreck.'

'Oh yeah. They were all diving round the wreck, that part is fact. But what he probably didn't tell you, it wasn't the ship's fabric they were plundering. It has been used to hide drugs. They still don't know where they come in from. But the divers go off from the main harbour and use that small boat to drop the stuff off, hiding it somewhere around the rondavel. Then they return to the harbour and come back to collect it from here when the coast is clear so to speak. Trouble is the locals found out what was happening and wanted a slice of the action. That's why they brought the dogs in, they knew there would be stuff here. They also knew there would be a lot of guilty folk hovering around to collect it.'

'Bloody hell.'

'In the UK they have been looking into his neighbourhood dispute. As ever, it wasn't what he portrayed it to be. He was accusing the neighbours of excessive noise, unreasonable behaviour, that sort of thing.'

'Yeah, that's what it sounded like. Minor inconveniences I thought.'

'Well, they have interviewed the neighbours. A bit cagey they were. But on deeper investigation it would appear it was drugs related. They're not quite sure who was dealing what. Or perhaps who was not paying for what. They've had surveillance on both houses. Quite a few visitors to Mark's place during his absence! Then the question of his identity came up. They thought he was phoney. It wasn't until we found the passports that I knew we could fill in the missing link for them. Craig Daniels is a known trafficker. And what's more, they think the stuff was going back in your suitcase.'

Fiona rattled her cup back on its saucer.

'OH MY GOD.'

She pulled her cardigan around her. Her arms hugged her body as she sank back into the chair closing her eyes.

'Will you excuse me for a moment?' Ennis spoke.

Fiona opened her eyes and nodded. She began rocking to and fro in the chair. Rocking to conceal her shaking.

When Ennis returned he asked, 'Is Ted Grant any relative of yours? Actually that is a daft question, there are hundreds of Grants aren't there?'

'Why?'

'Oh there's a photo on the wall by the gents. A Ted Grant caught the biggest marlin on the coast many years ago. But the record still holds today.'

'Really?'

'Yes.'

'And?'

'Well.' Ennis fiddled with the keys in his safari suit pocket. 'I think it's about time we were going.'

'Hang on. What about this Ted Grant?'

'Go and have a look for yourself.'

Ennis followed Fiona to the bank of photographs and pointed out the one of Ted Grant.

'Oh' was all Fiona could find to say.

'There is a rumour that he left the country under a cloud. He always maintained his innocence, but the powers that be are convinced that he was party to some very shady land allocations. There were a couple of unexplained incidents... dead bodies, but no one ever got to the bottom of it. In the middle of the investigation he disappeared and has never been seen since.'

Fiona didn't think it appropriate to mention her grandfather, he'd never gone into any detail about the place, just how fantastic it was.

'The wreckage,' Ennis said pointing in the direction they had come from, 'that wreckage, went down at about the same time. No survivors were ever found.'

'Do they think he was escaping by boat?'

'No one has ever said.'

Fiona looked back at the photo, trying to make out any

distinguishing marks in the old grainy image, trying not to look as if she was too concerned about the story.

'Let's go. You are booked on tonight's flight. I will be escorting you.'

'Why all the fuss?'

'Fiona, it's just the way it is going to be. I assured Chris you would be safe.'

She knew enough about the workings of the police that there was a problem. Just now she was not sure she wanted to know what it was. Her stomach churned, as she breathed in the salt laden air. Memories of her first boat trip as a child came flooding back. She was eight. It was a holiday treat. Her grandfather was at the helm of a small fishing boat. It was rough, the boat was heaving from side to side. She was sick, very sick. She could still see her grandfather's face looking out to sea with grim determination, so determined she was going to like the sea, convinced he could instil sea legs into her.

Fiona looked up at Ennis; his face had a similar look of determination on it.

Llansteffan Beach

Llinos Jones

A view to inspire, surely?
A vista too wide for one pair of eyes
As April shines on a rare kind day.

Breeze-blown and sunburnt, I'll plead for your
words
To soar, vulnerable and unbound by
The restraints of your withered ambition.

But this mission to reconcile the heart and mind
fails;
My drowning love, your airy words, too distant to
agree;
A petty dissonance to spoil the eyes' indulgence.

Your eyes scan the structured streets of Ferryside
Their blank stares traversing the estuary.
I look up and view the sun,
Haloed through your hair.

Yet we walk to the shore, disappointed at
The sea, a murky blur in the distance.

The beach lies first in acres,
Corrugated and whipped by squally sunshine;
Moulded waves limping to the sea.
We sink in clammy sand
Which socks our ankles in dampness, sucks our
paces to stumbles
Through the dead confetti of open shells underfoot.

True Colours

Katy Griffiths

She rang up last Saturday, when Grace was out, so they
didn't have a chance to speak. Initially Grace was grateful
for that, it gave her time to absorb the shock, time acting
as a buffer, a cushion, like falling through feathers. Mia was
good at shock tactics, primarily because they were her only
tactics and she would no doubt have enjoyed hearing Grace
at the other end; the sharp intake of breath, the clunk as
the phone hit the floor, the prolonged silence as her whole
body froze and she waited for it to come back to life. And
she would have frozen. She knows she would because that's
exactly what she did, when she heard that message coming
through on the answer phone; this metallic, sharp distorted
voice, which didn't sound anything like Mia at all. But then
that was often the case with technology; you never sound
like yourself, which was fitting for Mia, as she was rarely

herself, even when acting like herself, with acting being the operative word. Maybe this was an act too; the message, the contrite apology; the assumption of friendship. It might be nothing, just empty words, hollow and vacant and echoing round the walls. It might be all those things, and numerous others too, but she needed to find out.

She almost wished she could have been there to answer the phone; it would have given her the chance to slam the receiver down dramatically, as in novels, as in films, closing the book, shutting the door and imagining the look on Mia's face at being on the receiving end of a thunderous 'no'. It wouldn't have worked though, Mia never took no for an answer with anybody, but especially not with Grace, who she could wear down, grind down, guilt trip into doing anything, as she had done so many years ago. At any rate, it would have been better than hearing the message, which was so much worse than hearing Mia in person. It was like having a little piece of her floating around in the atmosphere, distilled and distorted, niggling at her constantly, nibbling and gnawing her way through into her mind, under her skin and back into her good books. Although that wasn't going to happen now. No way, she could forget that. She didn't have any good books left for Mia; they'd all been thrown away.

The message had been vague, but not quite vague enough. Typical Mia, leaving little hints and trails, reeling you in, weaving her little web and wrapping you up inside it. It was so easy for her and what made it easy was that she knew Grace. She knew her inside out, back to front, upside down and round about. Never give the enemy too much information. Well, that's easy when you know who your enemy is, but all of this information was gleaned before she knew she was an enemy, before her true colours started coming through, loud and clear. But she knew Grace well enough to leave the right hint; she knew which buttons to press, levers to pull. She knew the card which would up the stakes and it was played quite casually at the end of the message.

'Oh, by the way, I wanted to speak to you because, well, it's all a bit silly really but... well, you see I'm getting married in the summer and I'd really like you to be...' The machine clicked off, leaving Grace hanging by a thread, both twisting and turning in the breeze.

Married. She was getting married; Mia was getting married. To Stuart, she wondered inwardly. Oh God, what if it was Stuart. What if she was marrying Stuart? It might not be Stuart. Hardly. It couldn't be Stuart. But what if it was?

She knew why Mia had done it, she knew she'd said it because she knew that one would hurt, and it did hurt; the pain throbbing its way through her insides, forcing itself out when once, she'd shut it all away. The wondering hurt more than anything, the question mark, the speculation, the doubt. She could have just told her, said his name, got it over with, but no; Mia has to leave her wondering, leave her hopeful, leave her hanging, preferably over a cliff edge, with a thinning rope and hordes of ravening serpents underneath, snapping at her heels. And the worst of it was that Mia would just leave her there, just keep her suspended, revolving in the ether, clinging and crawling with every last breath, until finally, just before the rope snapped and she fell to her fate, Mia would reach out a hand and offer salvation, resolution. It was only at that point, at that moment, that Mia would throw her a lifeline and answer the question that lay between them like a bolster, offering little comfort and keeping them consciously separate, as they had been for the last eight years. She wouldn't be able to say anything; she couldn't ask, couldn't request; couldn't go crawling to Mia on her hands and knees, with her dignity waiting at home, begging to know whether he was still under her spell or if it had been broken. But she needed to know. Her brain was reeling just thinking about it, spinning and staggering over itself, reinvigorating all her memories of angered sorrow and confused pain, which returned to her now seemingly stronger and with more sting after all those years lying dormant; the serpent's tail still flickering. She couldn't be marrying Stuart. A picture of them together formed inside her brain and she dismissed it with a flick of her hand, sending them off the cliff and into the ocean. No she couldn't be; that all happened years ago and Mia wasn't exactly keen on long term relationships. No, she'd have cast him out a long time ago. It couldn't be Stuart.

But she had to know. And that's what Mia knew.

The inside of the bar looked worse than the outside. The smoky interior filled with zebra skin settees and leather chairs didn't exactly exude good taste but still this was where Mia had asked him to meet. Stuart hesitantly peeped through the doorway, fear filling his stomach, as he edged further into the blackened room, sound bouncing off the walls and reverberating in his ear drums. He couldn't see her from where he was standing, which would have helped matters somewhat and made him feel better about entering the lion's den that seemed to lie before him, if he knew she had already arrived. But still Mia had asked him to meet her here and from whatever compulsion had gripped him at the time, he didn't feel like he could refuse now. Grace was working tonight, so it was highly unlikely that she was going to walk in. Still, this horrible feeling continued to hover over him, like a grey, heavy cloud passing over, getting darker and darker and threatening to rain. He didn't know why he was getting so worried about this; Mia was Grace's friend, her best friend in fact; she wasn't going to mind about him meeting up with her best friend, surely? Guilt pressed down on him further, forcing itself into his consciousness and whispering all the things he didn't want to hear, giving him the almost continual feeling that he was being watched. There was nothing wrong with what he was doing. Still, that didn't explain why he hadn't told Grace what he was doing tonight, why he said 'oh, nothing much really,' instead of admitting the truth, that he was meeting up with her best friend for a drink. More to the point, it didn't explain why Mia hadn't told Grace either, which gave him even more reason to fear the unknown path in front of him. He hadn't really thought much about it at the time, her effectively asking him out, but along with the realisation that she hadn't told Grace about this meeting, a certain dark fear had started to creep in. What was she expecting? What did she want?

He moved further inside the room, slowly, taking hesitant mini steps, looking furtively about him to see if he could detect any familiar faces. Not that it mattered if he did see anybody, of course. It was only a drink, after all, with Mia, with the beautiful, charming Mia. But then, if anybody did see him and told Grace, well, it might give the wrong impression, especially as he hadn't told her. And it would be the wrong impression, of course. What other impression was there to give? 'We're friends aren't we?' That's what Mia had said. 'What could possibly be wrong with two friends going for a drink?' She'd smiled as she said it, revealing perfect teeth between two red stained lips, almost the exact same shade as the varnish on her perfectly manicured nails. Stuart didn't quite know what to say to this, having no idea what reply he could possibly form, with his mouth drying up and his vocal chords twittering. He wouldn't have said they were friends, exactly. She was Grace's friend, but that didn't make her his friend, except in a distant way, a sort of friend-once-removed. But he didn't wish to offend her in any way, so he simply nodded, aware that some vague form of English would fall from his lips, as it often did when Mia was in the vicinity. 'W... W... W... Well, yes... I suppose...yes, you could say... I imagine we must... be friends.' It had all been quite casual really; the asking out, if you could call it that, which of course you couldn't, he couldn't, as that would imply a date, and this wasn't a date. Nothing of the kind. Ridiculous suggestion, which didn't explain why his palms were perspiring and his hair was somehow glued to his forehead. It was very warm in here though, he thought, glancing around at the myriad bodies filling the room. It couldn't be nerves making him feel this way. He wasn't nervous, why should he be nervous, it was only Mia, lovely, glamorous Mia. They'd all gone out together before; he, Grace, Mia and Adam. They'd all got on well together, mostly, though for his part he'd never liked Adam. He was too full of himself, too smarmy, too oily and grovelling. If he was chocolate, he'd have eaten himself. Mia deserved somebody better than that. He wondered if she'd told Adam about tonight, and his resolve suddenly weakened, combined with a waitress in fishnet tights suddenly accosting him out of nowhere, intruding on his thoughts and asking him if he was meeting someone tonight. 'No, no,' he said, his voice suddenly several octaves higher than he intended. 'I'm not meeting anybody. Why would you think that? Why should I be meeting anybody? I'm just here for the music.' Panic seemed to fill his body and he sprinted for the door, when suddenly Mia sashayed through it, beaming 'Stuart, how lovely to see you, sorry I'm late. Were you leaving?'

'No,' he said shaking his head, although his hair still refused to move. 'No, I was just... getting some fresh air. Dreadfully hot in here.' She smiled warmly and took his arm, leading him to the bar. Surely one drink wouldn't hurt.

Grace's hand hovered warily over the receiver, itching to pick it up, before something inside her, dignity perhaps, snapped it back and returned her hand to her mouth, where her nails were being steadily demolished. She wouldn't make the first step, she couldn't. That would display her interest, that would tell Mia she'd won, with her devious words having worked their way into Grace's brain, pushing all the right buttons along the way, as she knew that they would. No, Grace said to herself, an air of prompt decision descending; she would wait. She would both wait and make her wait. If Mia wanted to talk to her, she would ring back;

if she was that keen to gloat, to rub it in, to slice the wound that little shade deeper. It wasn't up to Grace to make the first move, or second, with Mia having checkmated her from the very beginning. She sat down on the settee, staring at the telephone, like watching a ticking time bomb and waiting for the explosion. She wondered if Mia was doing the same thing, sat at home, waiting, watching, wanting, poised and ready to pounce. She doubted it, Mia never waited for anybody, or anything; she just blew in and took what she wanted, scattering all those that got in her way and leaving others to clear up the carnage. That was Mia distilled to her essence, though of course not many people saw that side; her real side, her best side, depending on the angle, or the poses. Mia rarely showed her real nature to anybody, except those she really liked; the side which seemed to be composed of all the bad characteristics of several human beings put together, as if she had lined them all up and sucked out all the rotten, leaving behind empty cadavers, with dazed expressions and manic grins. That was the bad side of Mia, when she was Mia the planner, Mia the plotter, Mia the snake, although she did have a good side, with each showing themselves alternately whenever charm or anger was called for. There was little in between with Mia; she was like a silver grey cat, either lying prostrate across your lap, purring softly, or out on the prowl, her tail was up and twitching back and forth, claws out and ready to strike. Grace had little doubt which side she displayed to Stuart.

She continued sitting there, eyes fixated on the phone, though she was still in her coat, still in her shoes, still with that same paled expression since the colour had drained from her face upon hearing that voice creeping through the ether. She shook her head, getting up and wandering into the kitchen, making a determined effort to drag her mind elsewhere, however unwillingly it clung to the telephone and demanded to be forcibly removed. She was doing exactly what Mia wanted; she was falling into her trap, which threatened to whisk her up at a moment's notice, leaving her suspended, hanging, falling. She was letting her in again, and she couldn't do that. She had to slam the door, batten down the hatches and bar all the windows. She couldn't let her get back in. She had too much to lose now.

Mia continued to stare out of the window, watching the world float past her in an indistinguishable blur. She wasn't used to this, being driven, being taken anywhere, but here she was, sitting in the passenger seat of Stuart's car being driven to the back end of nowhere. She didn't like this, sitting in the passenger seat when she was used to being the driver, used to being in control, and controlling. This wasn't her style, not at all, but here she was. Not that she had a choice, of course, but it wouldn't be for long. Give it a few days, a few weeks, a few months at best, and then it would all be over. It wouldn't last; they never did. Not that it was her fault, but men seemed to lose their appeal once the battle was won and she could carry them home like a trophy, though obviously not to keep on her mantelpiece, gathering dust. She felt bad about Grace, of course she did. How could she not? They were friends, after all. Of a sort. Vaguely. Friends but with reservations; a detached form of friendship, distant, conducted from opposite sides of the room, with distinctly drawn lines across the middle and trenches optional. That wasn't friendship, Mia reasoned, not real friendship, not true, loyal, honest friendship. Most friends would be standing in the middle of the room, gossiping and giggling, heads together, spilling their secrets; Mia always viewed Grace from the opposite wall, cool and aloof, with a drink in her hand. That was the trouble, she thought, as the verdant blur of emerald hedgerows gave way to the greying stonework of the motorway; they were always on opposite sides of the room.

Mia turned her thoughtful face away from the window, glancing instead at the beaming face of Stuart, hands clasped firmly on the driving wheel and pasting on a smile as he turned to look at her. It was amazing, she thought, how he seemed to have changed since they left, transformed even, lifted. It was as though all the events of the past few weeks had been lying heavily on his shoulders, and now that they were finally gone, all that weight had just floated away, drifting throughout the atmosphere, swooping and falling like seagulls, and suddenly he had returned to his full height, breathing in fresh new air, unlike the dogged, leaden, smoke filled oxygen that had been forcing him down and pulling him under. He was even changing gear with more confidence, driving with that laid back, leisurely air of self assurance, which was no doubt intended to look impressive, but was driving Mia slowly mad. She gritted her teeth behind her smile; he might as well just put one elbow out of the window and have done with it. But she smiled and smiled because she felt sadly responsible for this change in attitude. It was because of her that he was suddenly rejuvenated, revitalised, face-lifted without the surgery, and when he stared out at the road ahead of him, he wasn't just looking at where he was going, but gazing out at this brilliant new future, which was bright because she was part of it. And she hated him for it. Men are such fools, she thought, turning her face away from his sickeningly sunlit expression, requiring sunglasses to handle the glare. Was that why she did it? Maybe. The money? Maybe that too. The thrill? Possible. Imagining the look on their faces when they discovered an empty wardrobe and an equally empty suitcase? Maybe all of those things. Maybe she just wasn't good at relationships. Maybe she just didn't want to try.

The scenery had now changed back to the rich rural landscape, reduced to haziness, so she turned again to the window, unable to handle looking at Stuart any more, who was now actually whistling, he was so happy and carefree. She did Grace a favour, getting her away from him. Grace was worth so much more than that, she deserved somebody so much better, as did Adam, she reflected, her thoughts slowly drifting back. Of all the guys, she could perhaps have seen herself with him. Not that he was 'The One', or any other such drippy shit terminology, but she could have stayed with him. Maybe. Or maybe it would have ended badly, just like all the others, just like every other man she'd been with, who'd raised her hopes, only to dash them back down to nothing and then leave, with emptiness echoing. Again and again and again, just the same story permanently on rewind. She should have been getting used to it by then, should have noticed the signs, which were practically like bright neon flashing arrows, instead of just falling repeatedly into the same trap. Maybe she just wasn't a good judge of character; maybe she was just too trusting, back then, when she was young and immature, easy prey for more experienced predators, a limp rag doll ready to be moulded by others, forcing her into shapes she didn't want to take. She closed her eyes, letting the memories wash over like waves of nausea, watching them drifting out to sea, and then drowning slowly on the horizon. She didn't think about the past, determinedly dragging her thoughts, kicking and screaming, back to the present. What was the point? It didn't matter, not any more. Not since she decided to give up on all that, decided to bite back and take some control. She couldn't be bothered with all that relationship crap any more. What was the point? Obviously there were no good men, so she might as well just make the most of the bad ones, going into it eyes wide open and heart shut tight, sealed down like a fortress. Her subsequent research had provided conclusive evidence that there were no good men, she thought, glancing across at whistling Stuart, who she might have considered a good man once, having gained all the right points on a survey, answered all the right questions and ticked all the right boxes, but who was now driving off into the distance, happiness etched on his face, not thinking about the girl he had left behind, and the letter he had written, without care or attention, just a bare exposition of the facts. Not that she was bothered; she wasn't some naïve romantic who believed in the redeeming power of love. Love didn't get you anywhere, as far as Mia could see, except on this ring road to nowhere. Not that Stuart thought that, she reflected, as the annoyingly high pitched, cheery whistling bored into her brain. But still, he'd never know. And what you don't know can't hurt you. Not yet anyway.

She thought back to the letter, left lying casually by Grace's phone, a ticking time bomb just waiting to be detonated, and the similarly phrased one placed under Adam's door, which would no doubt self destruct in thirty seconds. They would probably get together later and compare notes, raking Mia over the coals; dissecting her, pulling her this way and that, turning her upside down and shaking her in the hope that the truth would fall out. She could picture Grace reading it, picture the destruction and the fallout that would come later, as Grace could never hide her emotions, leaving all the pages open and free to be rifled through, unlike Mia who was a closed book, bound up tightly, with chapters pulled out and rewritten several times over. She felt bad about Grace, of course she did. She didn't want to hurt her, of course she didn't. She didn't want to get too close, didn't want to let her in. She'd done her a favour, in the long run; getting her away from that simpering idiot of a boyfriend. She was too good for him; Mia could see that, from the very moment he came crawling up to her, leering and groping, unable to resist the pangs of temptation. He was a liar, a cheat, a fraud; she could tell that, the moment he agreed to come out with her for a drink that night. Grace deserved better than this stuttering fool, she resolved, brushing all other thoughts away from her mind. But she could still see her face. She could still see the letter, resting on the telephone.

Grace could still hear her voice, breaking through the telephone. No matter how much she tried to do something else, tried to occupy her mind, Mia still came filtering through. No matter how many times Grace tried to swat her away, how many barriers she put up, Mia still got through; an intrepid explorer, hacking through the undergrowth. Not that it was exactly uncharted territory; she'd wormed her way into Grace's psyche many times before, and at much closer ranges. And here she was again; trying once more, the final push, one last attempt at breaking down the defences, dropping the bombshell on an unsuspecting enemy. And that was the key feature, the element of surprise. No matter how Grace tried to protect herself now, she couldn't because Mia was already in; she'd already taken the territory; assembled her weapons and done her homework. It was no good. Grace could still hear her. Even though she'd been polishing the kitchen to within an inch of its life, she could still see Mia in every reflected surface. She wandered back into the dining room, intending to sort through a batch of magazines that had been resting on the coffee table for months, but yet again found herself staring fixedly at the telephone and yet again succumbing to pressing that button. She felt cold, hearing Mia's voice with its monotone, almost hypnotic quality, charming and enchanting you, like the snake that she was, casting a spell; luring you in, pulling you towards her, almost effortlessly, whilst Grace desperately dug her heels into the ground. The machine clicked off with that same deafening thud. She sat for a moment, curiosity gradually getting the better of her. She had to do something; she couldn't just sit here waiting for Mia to ring, look at the state she was in. Anyway, it was ridiculous, all this bluff and double bluff; they used to be friends, for heaven's sake. Grace picked up the telephone with a new resolve, and briskly dialled the numbers, her fingers rapidly running over the snow white buttons, before she suddenly stopped, slamming the phone down on the receiver, as her mind's eye pictured a letter, left beside a very similar telephone several years ago, and all her warmth towards Mia evaporated, leaving similar steam. She remembered how she felt when she saw that letter, when she read its contents and wanted to tear it up, ripping it into the shreds of a thousand pieces and imagining she was doing the same to those who had written it, whilst shades of embarrassment and stupidity floated over her. The emotions of the moment came flooding back to her, overwhelming her like a tidal wave. All she could hear were questions in her mind. How could she have not seen it? But she hadn't. How could Mia have done it? But she had. How could they have done it? But they had. The same facts came back to her, over and over, hitting her repeatedly on the forehead, as if to knock it into her head that it had actually happened. Whatever the questions, it was always the same answers. They were gone. Mia and Stuart were gone. Together. That was the end of the story, whatever the beginning might have been.

Grace sat back on the settee, the tidal wave having passed off, but the water still lapping at her feet; the memory of past pain lingering like scorch marks. She felt calm now, composed, collected. She knew what to do now, decidedly pressing the delete button, and sending Mia floating off into the ether, arms flailing and spinning into the vortex, without a backward glance. She had to do something. It wasn't up to her to make contact; Mia would find her way in anyway. She'd phoned Grace, she'd made the first move; she obviously wants something and when Mia wants something she always gets it. More to the point, she always knows how to get it, which was why Grace was so worried. She'd seen this so many times before, watching Mia plotting and planning, finding any chink in the armour and playing it for all it was worth. But what could she want now? Revenge? The very word sent a freezing chill down Grace's spine. She couldn't, she wouldn't, that was years ago, her and Adam. She didn't meant to; they didn't mean to, it wasn't as if it was planned, it just happened. She imagined herself trying to explain all that to Mia, and seeing her laugh, a deep throaty laugh, like a pantomime villain. She wanted to tell her, wanted to be honest, wanted to explain; it wasn't just some sordid little fling, she loved him. But Mia didn't give Grace a chance to explain, she didn't say much at all when she found out about them both, which terrified Grace more than anything. Actions clearly speak louder than words. Anyway, why did she need to explain herself to Mia, now, of all people, after what she'd done with Stuart? Why would she want to know about this now? What could she possibly want? Who could she possibly want? Not Adam. She wouldn't, she couldn't. They were still together, they were still here. She couldn't imagine Mia was still with Stuart, she didn't love him like Grace loved Adam. She didn't mean to do it; she didn't mean to hurt Mia. She couldn't help it, they couldn't help it. They didn't mean to. It just happened.

The phone rang. The shrill ring bit into her thoughts, running through her body like a jolt of electricity. She stared at the phone. Was it? Could it be? She didn't want to, she couldn't face her, but whatever it was, she couldn't hide. Not now, not when Mia was already on the trail, smelling the scent and following her nose. She didn't want to, but recognising she didn't have any choice, Grace slowly, and with shaking fingers, gingerly picked up the receiver, praying she didn't recognise the voice on the other end.

Bright Lights, Big City

Jessie Ledbetter

Los Angeles stopped suiting Claire Bennett when she was seventeen. There were too many lights, the sun was too bright; too many fake, perfected Barbie dolls walked the streets, the sand at the beaches was too dirty, the air too polluted. Feeling trapped in the world's greatest paradise, Claire fought her way through her remaining year of high school and the four years of college at UCLA, as her parents refused to pay out of state tuition. When that diploma was handed to her in its shiny little black case, however, Claire Bennett backed up her '97 Saturn and turned her back on LA, no intention to ever return.

So when her mother had called this morning, hysterical, Claire, who now called herself Cecilia, had stubbornly refused. She'd refused on the phone the first time and the second time and the third time her mother had called, panic heavy in her voice. It wasn't until her brother called, his deep voice putting a taste of sour milk in the back of her mouth, that Cecilia had finally given up and submitted.

Now that she was here though, she was beginning to think she should have held firm.

Los Angeles airport was as ridiculous as it usually was; she found that she still hated the surging mass of people, the inconsistencies between the tropics-like atmosphere and the self centred, all-for-the-one-me, attitude disgusting. She was shoved out of the way by some want-to-be actor and shoved back, not at all afraid of offending anyone in this god forsaken city.

'Bitch,' he said through his mock designer sunglasses and Cecilia raised a finger, cocking her head and smiling sickly. He rolled his eyes but moved and she was able to grab her bag.

She moved to the Avis Car Rental desk, rented some cheap piece of shit car that would probably die on her halfway through the canyon but what the fuck did she care? She didn't even want to be here.

When she'd left LA, she'd headed straight to Seattle, the city with the country's highest suicide number. Seattle, Claire knew, would be the greatest place for her. Rainy, depressing, full of want-to-be poets and writers, away from the bright lights of the Hollywood sign and not a billboard in sight. She found Seattle to be everything LA wasn't and settled in with something close to euphoria.

In Seattle, Claire got to be anyone she wanted to be – so she became Cecilia, a woman who dyed her hair jet black and wore it straight to her shoulders with straight, thick bangs and thick rimmed glasses. She wore black fingernail polish and wore greys and blacks and nothing else. Occasionally, she'd throw in a red scarf if she was feeling particularly frisky, but no one questioned the black, no one demanded colour because in this city of rain and rain and rain, all they knew was sleet, black, gray, mist, and fog.

She worked for a small printing house that published mainly depressing poetry written by poets who were on the verge of suicide themselves; Cecilia couldn't get enough of it. Her enthusiasm, her love of the form and her obvious ability to seek out new, brilliant talent moved her quickly through the ranks so when her mother called hysterically that morning, Cecilia's office door's plaque said Junior Editor.

Driving in LA was like entering a street race with no hopes of a monetary prize if you survived. Luckily, death got stuck in traffic like everyone else and Cecilia managed to squeeze her way onto the 405 before it merged with the 5, heading towards Santa Clarita, which hadn't existed when Claire had lived here; then, Cecilia thought, it had been called Valencia and it had still belonged to Mother Nature.

The sun shone and the thermometer in the car read 78 degrees despite it being the middle of February. Cecilia shrugged out of her coat and dug around in her bag for the cheap pair of sunglasses she'd grudgingly bought from the stand in LAX airport; after all, she thought with a bitter shove of her finger as she rolled the window down, when the hell would she ever need sunglasses in Seattle?

The drive took her over an hour and by the time she managed to pull off the 5 and onto McBean Drive, her sweater was plastered to the back of her and the seat of her trousers felt sweaty and sticky.

The hospital was close, thank God, and Cecilia parked the rental car as close to the door as she could. Inside, the air conditioning was pumping like a well oiled Crew member, keeping the crisp, antiseptic air at a steady 65 degrees. Claire tossed the sunglasses into her bag as she approached the receptionist.

'I'm looking for Harry Bennett,' Cecilia said to the woman.

Without looking up, the nurse scanned her lists. She raised one finger, long, with a fake nail that was painted a flaming shade of orange, and pointed to the right. 'Room 134.'

Cecilia made her way down the hall, her chunky boots adding their own rhythm to the steady beat of heart machines and breathing bags. 134 was at the end of the hall and with a deep breath, Cecilia shoved the door open.

'Claire!' her mother cried as soon as she entered, smothering Cecilia in what appeared to be a giant white bat but which was actually an overly large wrap containing the petite, plastic and manicured Diane Bennett.

Cecilia managed to separate herself from her mother with great difficulty, gazing around the perfectly groomed middle aged want-to-be, and saw the room was plain, simple, white, too bright, and contained a single bed with two machines steadily working away. In the bed lay her father, his eyes closed, his skin almost as white as the room around him, not moving, the only sign that he still lived being the steady and constant buzz of the machines.

By the windows leaned her brother, the prodigal son, his arms crossed over his buff chest, his tight jeans designer quality, his hair shaggy and long, the perfect shade of copper blond. 'Claire,' James said with a raised brow, gazing at her distinctly unorthodox outfit of black.

'The doctors don't know what caused it, he's as healthy as a horse, they think it's his arteries but I don't believe that, he's been running for an hour every morning for the past five years, you know your father, determined to outlive Schwarzenegger, but I swear...'

'Mom,' James said, coming forward.

Diane put her hands up, her fake nails a pretty pearly pink colour that turned Cecilia's stomach. 'Right, right, sorry, I'm just so frazzled,' she said, looking anything but.

'They don't think he's going to live,' James said in that matter of fact way of his which made him such a great financial banker and Cecilia was sure made him so unappealing to the women who stuck around long enough to get a look into his head along with the look down his trousers. 'We wouldn't have bothered you except that this may be it.'

'I really don't want him dying with you still mad at him sweetie,' Diane said, coming forward and placing her hands gently of Cecilia's shoulders. 'The doctors think he can still hear so if you want to say anything...'

Cecilia shoved off her mother's hands. 'I'm here, don't push me,' she all but growled. She tossed her coat and bag into the chair by the door then put her hands on her hips. 'How long are they giving him?'

'He's in a coma right now but the longer he's unresponsive, the less time we have.' James shrugged a shoulder, resignation all over his face. 'So, at best a few days, at worst a few hours.'

'If only he'd wake up!' Diane said, wringing her hands. 'He's too young to go yet...'

'He's sixty nine,' Cecilia said flatly.

'That is still really young! Just because he waited a bit to marry and have kids doesn't mean he isn't still in the prime of his life...' Diane looked anything but heartbroken.

Cecilia shook her head. This was exactly why she never came back. 'I'm getting coffee.'

'What? No, no! I'll get you some coffee, James can come too, you should have a few moments...' Diane looked hopefully at Cecilia.

'No, I'm getting my own coffee.' Cecilia moved to the door before they could stop her and pulled it open.

Stupid, she yelled at herself all the way down the hall. How stupid did one have to be? She swore, on her life, that she would never return to this fucking state and what had she done? Bought an outrageously expensive plane ticket and hopped on, racing back to this fucking place because her stupid mother had cried and cried and her brother, who she hadn't talked to in years, had called to ask as well...

Cecilia shoved open the cafeteria door and nearly knocked a doctor to his feet. He grabbed the swinging door and moved his head, all the while holding the giant mug of steaming coffee away from himself.

'Sorry,' Cecilia said, actually feeling bad for her anger. 'That was a bit harder than I'd intended.'

'No, don't worry about it,' the doctor said with a smile. His eyes were old, much older than his middle aged body, and his hair was thinning but he looked oddly familiar...

And then Cecilia knew where she'd seen him before and the bottom fell out of her stomach and her skin turned clammy. Of course he would still be here, he was a doctor, they had to keep working, even though it was nine years ago, nine fucking years ago...

The doctor narrowed his eyes and cocked his head a bit. 'Do I know you?'

Cecilia nodded, though reluctantly.

And then his eyes widened and the smile slipped from his face. 'Claire Bennett.'

'I call myself Cecilia now.'

He nodded, shutting the door quietly. 'And how have you been?'

Cecilia felt like shoving her hands in her pockets or punching something but she didn't. The shame racing through her, the embarrassment, the memories she was forcibly locking down her throat with a thick pool of saliva, made it difficult to answer. 'Fine, just fine. Life's good, life's great, getting on with things.'

The doctor nodded, a little too knowingly, then the smile returned even though it was a bit sad. 'Glad to hear it. I've got to get back, but...'

'No, no, go please, sorry,' Cecilia said, moving out of the way.

He paused a moment longer, gazing at her. 'Take care, Ms Bennett.'

Cecilia nodded, closing her eyes when he left.

She got coffee, made her way back to her father's room. Her mother was leaning over the bed, the ever attentive want-to-be widow, and James stood by the window, his arms crossed over his chest as usual. Cecilia took the chair where her stuff sat and all but gulped the scalding caffeine down.

'Honey buns,' Diane was whispering sweetly, 'Claire's here, come on Harry, Claire's come home...'

'I'm not home,' Claire said loudly. 'And my name's Cecilia now.'

'Is that legal yet?' James asked without looking back.

'Yes.'

'Harry, honey, come on darling, open your eyes, talk to Claire, come on sweetheart...' Diane smoothed the stubble on Harry's cheek but he didn't stir. She managed to drop a few tears which slid down her botoxed cheeks quite smoothly, and Cecilia couldn't stomach it much longer with all this hoopla, how could they do it, this is madness, just let the man die with a moderate amount of decorum...

No, that darker side of herself said, the part that was still bitter, still angry. Let him die without dignity, let him rot in the ground, I hope the worms eat him alive...

The door opened and a doctor entered. He checked the charts, scanning Harry's progress, then looked up at Diane with grim eyes. 'I'm sorry, Mrs Bennett, it doesn't look good.' He looked around the room, noticing Cecilia's presence. 'You all might wish to say your goodbyes. I don't think he's got much more time.'

'Oh doctor, isn't there anything we can do?' Diane asked tearfully.

'Yeah, call the insurance company,' Cecilia muttered under her breath. James glared at her sharply and she raised a brow.

'I'm sorry, Mrs Bennett,' the doctor said, laying a gentle hand on Diane's shoulder. Then he left, shutting the door quietly behind him.

'You want to go first, Claire?' James asked, deliberately turning and staring down at her with his contact-blue eyes. 'Or are you too much of a bitch now to care?'

'Me, the bitch?' Cecilia stood but Diane rushed forward, placing herself between them.

'Now your father is dying, we are not going to do this here where they can hear...' she motioned to the door where the nurses walked by on watch.

'We're not going to do this at all,' Cecilia said. 'I should never have come.'

'Damn fucking right,' James said, tossing his head. 'You could care less about any of us, could you?'

'Yeah, and you care so much for me too, James, don't you, all those nice phone chats and family visits I get,' Cecilia said sarcastically. 'You are just the emblem of family love, aren't you?'

'Stop this,' Diane hissed, glancing at the door. 'Claire, let's give James a minute, a son should get to say goodbye to his father...'

'Yes,' Cecilia said with a roll of her eyes. 'The son should, of course the son should. One more baseball chat, eh, James?'

'Fuck you,' James seethed and Cecilia would have retorted but Diane shoved her out the door and into the hall.

'Now really, please,' Diane said, her hands shaking as she raised them to run them over her hair. Cecilia pretended not to notice. 'You should be nicer to your brother, Claire dear, he really does love you...'

'Loves me, does he?' Cecilia shook her head. 'Just like you love me too, right Mom? Just as long as I don't fuck up your perfect silicone world, right?'

'Claire, honey, no need to be nasty, that was a long time ago, we've all moved on, it's not worth dragging it all back out again...'

'Yeah, we've all moved on. Fuck you.'

Diane opened her mouth but couldn't seem to think of anything to say. She wrung her hands together, twisting her rings around her fingers. 'Your uncle, he's not coming.' She looked at Claire with pleading eyes. 'James refused to let lilii come.'

Cecilia shook her head. 'Great, fantastic Mom, that's exactly what I needed to hear, thanks so much, now everything's peachy.'

Diane scanned the hall, noticed the nurses moving towards them. 'Can we go outside for a moment, I need some fresh air.'

'Have at it,' Cecilia said, stalking off to the waiting room.

Cecilia stood surrounded by cheap plastic chairs, kicking one for good measure. Her mother had no right to bring it back up. No right at all. It wasn't hers to screw around with, was it? And mentioning what James had done...

Where did James come off anyway, it's not as if he'd been there, not once he'd hit college, they'd never seen him, just the tuition bill; it's not as if he'd ever cared, not enough to come home and see them once in a while, not enough to come when she'd needed him most...

He'd promised; the bile rose once again in Cecilia's throat and she swallowed hard. He'd promised, again and again, when they were kids, when the sky was full of stars and their sleeping bags were wet with dew, he'd promised, always he would be there, never would she have to be alone...

Fuck him, Cecilia thought turning back to the door. Fuck

them all. They'd turned their backs on her, washed their hands of her, just as she'd done to them. California was just a sweltering pot of sin and destruction, she'd escaped hadn't she? She was finished with this fucking place...

She paced back out to the door leading into her father's room and stood, staring through the small window at James. He was holding their father's hand between his own and saying something quietly, running a finger along the hairy backside of Harry's wrist. Then he leaned forward and with his eyes closed kissed Harry gently on the forehead. When he pulled away Cecilia was surprised to see tears coursing down his cheeks. He turned then, noticed her watching and stood quickly, yanking the door open. 'Your turn,' he growled, shoving by her and heading to the door.

Cecilia let the door close, heard the lock click. She stood in the hallway for a good long while, just staring at the door, before she finally pushed it open and went inside.

It was worse being in here alone with him, she thought, as she paced to the window and stood, fidgeting. At least with James and Diane in here she didn't have to look at him, didn't have to listen to her own thoughts; she could be mad at the lot of them, hating them all as she'd done so vehemently for so long. But now, with her father lying there helpless, all but dead, on the bed, the monitor quietly beeping at her, a gentle reminder that this was it, this was her last chance to say what she really felt...

'I hate you,' she said, surprising herself. 'I've hated you for so long I'm not sure why I even came. I've hated you for what you did, for all that you were. I hate you for turning your back on me,' she hissed. 'Of all people, you turned on

110

me, chose not to believe me, shunned me. And I fucking hate you for it.'

She pushed off the window ledge, moving closer to the bed. 'I told you what he did to me, I told you how Uncle Luke touched me, hurt me, I cried on your shoulder because I thought you'd protect me, you'd fix it...' Cecilia felt the old shame ramming its way from deep in her belly and fought it back. 'Instead you shoved me away, blamed me. Shouldn't wear such short skirts, Claire, you said to me, shouldn't dye your hair blond, shouldn't flirt like that. Isn't that what you said to me? Didn't you tell me it was my fault? Isn't that how you phrased it?' Disgust was a bitter bile on the base of her tongue and Cecilia wanted to retch, wanted to puke all her hatred for Harry out all over those clean, bright white sheets, but she bit down hard on her tongue and instead stood there, looking at the frail, greying, decomposing mass that had once been a father she'd adored, a father who had held her hand and her heart, a father who'd been a superhero... she stood there for a long time, simply watching him, before she turned and left the room.

She went to the parking lot, sat on a curb. She'd never smoked in her life but at that moment all she wanted was a cigarette. Her hands were shaking, her legs seemed to want to leap up and run and run, run away from here, run into the hills and to the brush, her fingers itched to light a fire and to lie on the ground and let the flames consume her, let them consume everything in this shitty little piece of paradise, eat away every person and every place and every memory... she didn't realise she was crying until she felt the tears on her hands, felt the salt on her tongue and then she was sobbing,

111

great racking heaves that ripped at her lungs and tore holes in her abdomen, that pushed her eyes from their sockets and made her nose all but a solid brick of mucus.

And then she felt a hand on her shoulder, hesitantly at first, then more firm, and then strong arms were wrapping themselves around her and she was leaning into someone, someone she thought might be the doctor, the doctor who'd been the only one to be nice to her throughout that whole ordeal, but no, it wasn't him, it was James, and James was there, finally, as he'd promised he would be when they'd been children, promised on those dark nights when they'd giggled, innocent as everyone starts out being, and he'd promised to always be the best big brother, to always protect her, and here he was, nine years too late...

But she let him hold her because she knew he needed this as much as she did. And she let him rub her back, let him hand her tissues, let him hold her hand when she was finally just hiccupping, let him help her to her feet and lead her back inside the hospital where they stood next to each other and watched as the doctors pulled the cords and their mother cried tears of anguish befitting the king of Jerusalem. They watched in silence as the body was covered in a white sheet and a nurse was sent to get Diane a sedative, something they both knew she'd see as her reward for such a brilliant performance.

'When are you leaving?' James asked the next morning as they sat on the curb outside the hospital, their eyes bleary from lack of sleep, the Starbucks in their hands a gift from James.

'Soon, I suspect,' Cecilia said, sipping the coffee that was anything but coffee.

James swallowed, once, twice, took a sip of coffee, shifted his boots. 'Perhaps...' he kicked a small rock, watched it roll down the gutter. 'Does Seattle have a nice season?'

Cecilia raised a brow. 'When it doesn't rain? Sometimes. In May.'

James nodded. 'I've got a few days of vacation coming up.'

Cecilia took a deep breath. 'We've got some great coffee in Seattle.' She looked down at the cup in her hand. 'Better than this shit.'

She thought she saw James's lips twitch. 'All right then.'

Cecilia nodded. 'All right.'

MIRAGE

Ghost in the Class Photo

Lucy Delbridge

Head all over
Dazed with deficiency
Colourless and vacant
Her dark eyes hollow caves
The usual excuses
Performed with efficiency
But time is running out for this ghost

Purple yellow pigment
Covers jagged bones
Senses fixed in winter
Mask the blazing sun
It's all such a big secret
But everybody knows
All she knows is that this could be the end.

Hair slicked back to cover thinning patches
Smile concealed by skinny lips
Baggy, spongy gums
Reality is distant

But reveals itself in snatches
And even she can see that this is wrong.

Flash, she is captured
An image for eternity
Everyone will remember
This is who she used to be
She can't see it yet
But she is her own enemy
And only she can save herself from harm.

Auschwitz

Jo Perkins

Quite soon
a face appears round the corner
of the red brick building.
Eyes sunken by anger and hunger
shackled by faded stripes.
Leaving no mark on the hard snow streaked earth,
she flits before the leering watchtower,
raises a finger to her lips, and disappears.

Driven by discomfort, we move on
trapped in the shuffling respectful crowds.
More clearly now she beckons
from the next doorway,
her floral dress flutters in the
draught, a coat loose about her,
her bare legs mottled, unfeeling.
She turns and checks the angle of her hat
in the smut streaked window.
We follow her along the concrete corridor
over the piles of shoes she scrabbles
for another pair, odd but even heeled.
She leads us past horror stained cells
and marches us over the frozen roll call ground.

She is waiting for us by the gas chamber
suitcase in hand,
not blinded by the winter sun
slicing low and cold through the thin trees.
She slips amongst us
as we walk free under the
metal lettered arch,
drab amidst our petrochemical hues.
She slides her hand inside the warmth of our jackets,
and her icy fingers encircle our hearts.

Oświęcim 2008

The House on the Border

Enid Smith

It's a lovely moonlight night;
                and hand in hand they go,
A gentle saunter up the lane, as bats fly to and fro.

The moon sails high above the ridge;
Outlines tall pines beside the house;
With stark remains thrust in the air,
Bare bones of what was once so fair.

A riffling breeze clangs old tin sheets,
The lovers cling together; then daring,
Heave a sagging gate, he pledges love forever.
Now carefully treading tumbled stones,
She gives a little giggle;
He risks a reassuring squeeze
With arm around her middle.

Through gaping windows wind pipes chill,
Then silence falls and all is still,
They hold their breaths, together cleave
A shadow falls – no sound from padded feet –

An eerie cry rings round the hill
And echoes round the heath;
The Hound of Hengest sounding death
To those who dare espy; Recalling legends
tales of old
Of Roman troops who conquered bold;
Broke ramparts built of rock and earth,
For keeping local tribesmen's worth,
Livestock, wives and children safe
Breached with marshalled troops in storm;
The leaders slain, the wives forlorn
And slavery became the norm.

Built hillside forts and metalled roads
And taught their patterns and their codes;
The Druid priests, torn, tortured slain
Temples raised to gods profane

'Til they left and Christians came – and changed
religion
Yet again.
And years of darkness, discord reigned.
Then heathen Saxons came to fight
Assailed once more with grasping might
To oust them dragon ships
Brought Viking hordes
And so the forts to castles turned
As people 'gan to rally – built little townships,
Inns and shops as drovers trecked their way
And horns called round the valley.

Through years of toil and little play,
Below the track, beside the ridge,
Of local stone the Hengest Manor home was born
Lush farms below, wild heath above,
With solid buildings shielded from
the Northern gales
And pine trees sheltering to the West –
A prosperous homestead 'til
His lordship riding from the bank –
His gallant hound beside
Was stabbed behind by robber band –
The hound leaped to defend but died to take a life;
His warm blood mingled with his lord's
And so the legends say
So where in taverns drovers met
To yarn and spread their tales
Legends grew and waned – as memories fade
Some believed and others saw and wondered
'Was it something in the ale? Did the undead ride
the ridge?
And was that weird unearthly cry The Hound
of Hengest
Passing by?' Presaging some untimely death from
unassuaged revenge?

By now our lovers have their fill –
Their fearful forms are frozen still,
Romance has died – the maiden cries;
'This place it bodeth ill –
Not for love you brought me here!

You hoped to gain your will by fear!
I will away – back to my bed –
Before I am but smitten dead!!'

She turned to run the way she came
But stumbled on the rubble.
The black hound screamed out in the night
The cry that heralds trouble;
Her lover turned and fled away
His sweetheart, silent, left to stay.

Grando Returns

Enid Smith

That Sunday they were going to a motor rally in Bradon Forest, about thirty miles away.

Alice was excited, bobbing up and down in her Timberland boots. Being two years older than Peter she was expecting to join up with several of her school friends and their families. Peter was worried, he hated the noise of revving engines and the screaming and shouting of crowds. He felt a cloud of misery coming down but supposed he'd have to grin and bear it.

He decided to wear his big welly boots and waterproof anorak, guessing it would be very muddy and probably wet.

Mum finished packing the food container, plenty of soft drinks, fruit, tomatoes and the sort of sandwiches he liked, some cheese and some of that spicy stuff, he could never remember what it was called. She reached for her long waterproof mac and began to button it; the middle buttons wouldn't fasten. Peter watched, fascinated:

'You *are getting* fat Mum,' he exclaimed, 'thought you were on a diet?'

'That's your new brother, or sister, growing in there.'

'Will you be laying an egg then?'

'Whatever gave you that idea?'

'Grando said his Mum had laid an egg!' he explained.

His mother burst out laughing and hugged him.

'You've been having those funny dreams again haven't you?'

Peter wriggled out of her embrace and ran outside.

His mother's eyes followed him but secretly she worried about her small son.

Alice and Peter in the back of the car started the thirty odd miles checking number plates and makes of car. Peter got irritated when his sister kept screaming in his ear.

'Don't yell so much,' he begged.

'I'm not yelling, just trying to get you to listen.'

'Oh! Girls are all the same shrieking and giggling for attention.'

'Shut up pig face or I'll tell...' Peter realised she was going to say 'Dad'.

'Get stuffed!!' and he bunged his fingers in his ears, the black cloud was coming back down. Somehow he could never call 'that man' Dad and now they were having another baby. What, he wondered, was going to happen to himself and Alice – would they still want them living with them, where would they go? – and the black cloud settled more heavily.

They reached the venue and parked in a big gravelled

clearing and turned into a car park. Most of the cars were family saloons or estates with a sprinkling of exotic looking sporting jobs with polished chrome, big lights and tonneau covers. Alice was delighted.

'When I grow up that's what I am going to buy!' pointing to a sleek motor in brilliant scarlet.

'Big 'ed,' muttered her brother but before she could retaliate they were whisked away along a needle strewn path between the trees. The place they chose to stand was by a sharp bend on the motorbike track with an immediate steep climb up a rocky slope. They joined several other family groups with young children and Alice was soon able to find one of her playground pals. Peter was alone in his day dreams, he didn't have many friends because he didn't like football and rough sports.

What he did like was playing his recorder, he felt he was getting pretty good with it and teacher had entered him for an exam. She had suggested he might like to take up the clarinet if he passed and with that and his love of painting and drawing it made his school time rewarding.

As soon as the first rider came along the track Peter knew he was going to hate it; the girls began to screech and shout, the crowd pressed closer, especially when the rider revved loudly as he took the bend up the rocky bit. The next rider skidded a bit on the bend and it began to get muddy.

The next two both wobbled a bit as they skidded through the mud, spraying a few globs over the crowd who cheered madly at their favourites, revving fiercely with wheels spinning, giving off clouds of blue smoke to mingle with the crowd now yelling advice.

'Give 'er more revs! Put your foot down! Take it gently,' and so on.

Another rider came whizzing along, put his foot down to take the bend, and suddenly a third rider skidded on on top and they both landed in a messy heap, bike wheels spinning and the crowd howling instructions as two stewards rushed onto the track and pulled them out of harm's way, Peter had disappeared. Nobody noticed.

He followed a narrow track through the thick fir trees, one hand in his anorak pocket, his fingers curled round his treasured pebble, and as he touched it it began to get warm, then it got hotter and from above came the sound of loudly flapping wings, like a gigantic pigeon. There was a crackling and a few small twigs and needles showered onto his head and there in front of him was Grando, all puffing and blowing out steam like an engine as he flapped and folded his wings.

'You can fly!' Peter cried, 'When did you learn that?'

'As you can tell I'm not very good, my wings aren't really big enough yet and I get s-o-o out of puff. All dragons have to learn to fly as they grow, they have to go out and fend for themselves. Think what a congestion there would be if they all stayed at home.'

'But surely you need your mum to look after you, what about food and things?'

'Like baby birds, as soon as we can fly we have to start fending for ourselves, not like you humans, cosseted by your poor parents until you are nearly twenty. Besides there'll be an increase in the family soon.'

'How's that, your mum having a baby too?'

'You forgot, we're not humans, Mum's laid three eggs!'

'Three! That's a lot isn't it? Anyway where is the nest? Is she sitting on them?'

Grando hooted and spouts of steam shot out of his nostrils:

'Silly, course not – they just need a warmish place and moisture.'

'It wasn't silly,' Peter retorted. 'Birds always sit on their eggs to keep them warm, well, unless they're ostriches.'

'Never mind, if you promise not to tell anyone, I'll show you their hiding place.'

'Oh! Please.'

'Follow me – and be careful, the rocks are slippery.'

Grando led the way. Upstream a little way was a small waterfall, cascading in a showery spray into a dark gloomy pool.

'Hold onto my tail and don't let go' he ordered.

They slithered a bit on the gleaming rocks and Grando led them onto a narrow shelf, just wide enough for Peter's big feet.

There behind the waterfall was a little cave; they ducked at the entrance to get inside. Once there they paused while their eyes got used to the dark.

Gradually Peter was able to pick out a few small stalactites hanging from the roof and some tiny stalagmites growing up from the floor... and there... at the back of the cave, in a sandy dip nestled three greenish shiny eggs. They looked about the size and shape of a rugby football. He stepped forward.

'Don't touch them, they are very, very sensitive – the babies inside can hear and smell and they mustn't be upset, it's very bad for baby dragons.'

'Where's your mum?'

'Ah, she had to go out and find the supper. That's why I came back, to keep watch – and to see you – of course,' he added as an afterthought.

'What about your dad, can't he do that?'

'Huh! male dragons don't do things like that, besides I don't know who he is and I 'spect Mum has forgotten too!'

'So you don't really have a dad then?'

'No, we have a different way of life from humans. Male dragons don't look after eggs, or babies, not like your dad.'

'He's not my dad,' shouted Peter, red in the face, and humiliating tears oozed from his eyes.

Grando studied him for a moment then:

'With humans the father helps to look after the babies, and the older children – they have to – especially if they are married. You couldn't fly out and eat a dead lamb, or rabbit, could you? You'll see your new dad will look after you and your new baby when it comes. He's probably frightened you won't like him, which will make it hard to do the job properly. I'll bet he's really worried about you wandering off, probably got a search party looking for you by now.'

'You really think so?'

'Yes I do. Let's get out of here before they get police dogs sniffing around. I'm allergic to dogs.'

They scrambled out of the cave and over the slippery rocks.

Peter bent to tip some sand out of his boot and when he turned round Grando had gone and his silly sister was galloping down the path, screaming his name fit to frighten away all the dragons in the kingdom.

Within

Lucy Delbridge

I feel as though I'm in control
Yet it is me who is a slave
I feel strong and I feel powerful
Yet he makes me behave
It is something that I have to do
That sits under my skin
I am audience to the sermon
Of the demon, lies within

He makes me happy
Makes me pretty
He gets me through my day
He watches as you question
And he tells me what to say

He nourishes my self esteem
He quenches all my doubt
It is in my best interest
If he says I go without

He holds me and protects me
He keeps me safe inside
He shelters me from myself
Within him I can hide

Don't take him, I'll be ugly
I'll be ordinary me
He removes me from the average
Shows how special I can be

With him I'm happy
With him I'm pretty
I know, a slave I'll stay
He makes me who I want to be
With him I'll fade away...

D.N.R.

Caroline James

My feet skirt soft and smooth over frost tinged grass on square lawns. I am gliding on air towards the Promised Land. I see my goal in the distance; the land of promise and dream. It is high above sea level standing tall, proud and straight spires touch the stars above.

My mind is running fast, my body running slow, too slow. With every glide I am further away from my destiny. The intensity to see the Promised Land increases my activity and I hear far away voices calling me, beckoning me. Ahead the ghostly cloud forms the shape of a sacred woman in white, arms waiting, waiting for me.

The hills and valleys below comfort my soul as I drift into blue white oblivion. Snow tipped mountains, canyons and rivers beneath me as I glide smooth and soft. Hands outstretched, I reach for the silken wings of the albatross as he crosses my body; they flap effortlessly as he slips through my fingers and drifts away to nothing.

I see my peace, my wonderland of everything good and happy. Smiling I whisper 'I will soon be there, to lie and sleep'.

My words are smothered by the north wind blowing, sending me off course. The tall white spires are no longer in sight. My voice is lost in the wind; my arms lash out in cloud and I drift into darkness.

The light dims before me as I struggle to see ahead; Thick clouds block my view as I float into nothingness and beyond. Hope is fading with the light as I strain to see my lady. I am falling, falling through dark thick cloud and I want to fly with the grace of the albatross into my white peace. My guiding light of hope and tranquillity has gone.

My body is being rocked and pulled; pain is running through my limbs. My eyes closed tight refuse to open. The voices are back calling me shouting at me. I will not listen I will go to my destiny I am on the brink. My chest is heavy as gigantic thuds pound my weary body. I am nearly there and she is before me again. My lady is waiting, in the distance, peace and serenity.

Shooting pains drive up and into my body like glass daggers; my mind is not focusing any more. They are holding me back making me stay. I don't want to stay and try to see my Promised Land and my beautiful lady.

And she is gone, my pain is back; cold eyes open as I look at the masked faces surrounding my bed. They are smiling, talking, congratulating. My mortal body is back for the second time and I am weary and long for release. They wipe dribble from my thin blue lips.

Once more I scribble with bony fingers, no speech, D.N.R.... Please...

Shadow

Caroline James

Ghostly tentacles move
In hushed silence
Waiting, watching, listening,
Threatening
The stillness

Eyes bright, bulging, dart
Teeth bite into red lips
Quivering, shaking in
The stillness

It touches my soul, fear,
Hate, lust, torture.
Teasing and tantalising in
The stillness.

Jellied legs walk soft and slow
Into dark spheres of nothingness
It can smell and taste and touch
The stillness

Shuffling, scurrying, moving
Closer; flesh tingling; ripping skin on
Stony ground. Oozing Blood, throbbing
Pulsating vein; screams break
The Stillness

Just an Illusion

Katy Griffiths

The letter was framed in a glass case. Sally stared up at the words, written in such flowing calligraphic ink, on paper faded a crumpled russet, as if tea had been spilt over it and then dried in tones of pale chocolate. She willed her eyes to move away from it, but they seemed fixed, staring in dark oblivion at those words, every one reaching out and punching her in the stomach, shocking and shaking her world, like rumbles of dull thunder in the distance. All these years. All these years she'd been telling this story, saying those words over and over and Sally had never believed her. She wouldn't have believed her now, if she didn't have proof, if her eyes weren't seeing the very words she never wanted to accept; if her mind wasn't absorbing the very truth she never wanted to recognise. It was impossible. Sally glanced over the letter once more; her eyes seeing the words which her brain was failing to grasp.

Dear Emma... It feels like its been ages since I saw you last, though I know it was only a few days.... Hope that everything is well with you and Mary and your parents too.... I wish I could tell you more about what is going on here but I know they won't let me, though perhaps it's better that you don't know.... You wouldn't want to see the things I've seen.... I wouldn't want you to.... I wish I could get away from this place...

She hadn't really noticed it to begin with. She'd been interested more than anything. She'd never thought that it could be.... The title above the display case had drawn her: 'Letters from the Front Line in WWI'. The name had interested her, of course, but she'd never imagined... Emma, her grandmother's name. It couldn't be anything to do with her though, naturally. She never knew anybody...

The contents intrigued her as well. He obviously wasn't much of a writer, putting it together in fits and starts, but the emotion came flooding through, first through little gaps, little breaks, little chinks in the armour, then the deluge when the barricades finally fell. She jotted little sentences down in her notebook; good evidence, little titbits of human feeling she could work into her otherwise factual article. Perhaps the museum would let her have a copy, she thought, sliding the notebook back in her bag. She was about to move on, she might never have noticed.... But then she saw the other name, William Johnson, then another name, Mary. Her grandmother had a sister called Mary. Still, it couldn't be. No, she shook her head. It couldn't be. Then she read the little plaque they had placed underneath the letter, detailing how this letter hadn't been sent home, why he couldn't send it, and suddenly she grew cold all over, as if someone was standing behind her, enveloping her in ice. She staggered back from the display case. She couldn't believe it. She thought it was just in her mind, all in her head; an elaborate illusion, a mental fabrication. She'd always had a very creative grasp of the truth. She'd always loved telling stories, without any hint of reality within their walls. How was Sally to know that this wasn't another one?

'Once upon a time, there were two little girls, who lived in a small house, with a big garden at the back, where colourful flowers grew row upon row, called daffodils, begonias and roses. The two little girls had two little rabbits, one each, which their Father bought for them one birthday. They were called... Biscuit and... Barry. That's a nice name for a rabbit. They also had a pet dog called Bill, who was a sheepdog, even though they didn't have any sheep.

They lived in the house with their father and mother, who loved them very much. The littlest girl, called Mary, liked playing with her dolls best, but the eldest one, called Emma, liked to read books. She would sit in the corner chair, by the fireplace, with a book on her lap, and she would read and read and read, until it was time for her dinner, or tea, as she would only stop for food, or school. She liked to tell stories to Mary, though Mary was so little that she often didn't sit still long enough to listen. Emma was ten years old and Mary was only five. Emma wished she had a sister who was older than Mary, but then she wished for lots of things she couldn't have, so she didn't complain. Mary was old enough to go to school now, so Emma had to look after her, walking her down the long road through the village to their school. She didn't mind this too much. She could tell Mary her stories on the way in. Mary had to listen to her stories then.'

Emma folded back the scraps of paper, smiling as she examined her own childish scrawl, the illegibility owing to her speed and hurry in committing her thoughts to paper, before they flew out of her head, only to be replaced by others even more pressing. She had always had a very overactive imagination, creating pictures and forming words that bore no resemblance to reality. How seriously she took this scribbling when a youngster, sitting in her father's armchair when he was out at work, poring over books which were much too old for her, and then taking up paper and pencil under her bedcovers and attempting to emulate the styles of her literary idols.

How foolish they seemed now, she thought, gathering up the scraps of paper tied with string, and replacing them in her desk. How strange also, that the Emma and Mary of the stories were so strikingly similar to the Emma and Mary of real life. They did have a dog called Bill, but no rabbits, thank heaven. What terrible names to inflict on rabbits, Biscuit and Barry! She only wanted to call him Barry after Barry Benson, the schoolyard terror of her primary days. What a fitting revenge to give the name of such a bruiser to a rabbit! All her childhood stories were in a similar vein, all with herself in the leading role, though an idealised version of herself; herself as she would want to be but never quite had the courage; herself as she might be, if she had everything that she wanted. It wasn't really fiction, but her ideal world, where all the dreams she ever had came true and all the objections of her parents were brushed under the carpet, with Mary sitting comfortably by her feet as an objective, yet complicit, audience.

She thought of their more recent incarnations, the stories of her childhood reformed, revised and given breath before Sally, her adoring grandchild. Once more she had an audience, perched on her lap, ready and eager to hear, to believe, disbelieve and hear again, though even Sally's patience was failing now, no doubt disregarding all her tales of later life as the ramblings of an old woman, especially those concerning William.... She pulled the scraps of paper from the drawer and crumpled them within her wrinkled, age spotted hands, the sudden burst of anger giving them agility denied to them for years. She scrunched them into a rounded ball and aimed it at the waste paper basket, where it ricocheted off the woven willow with a limp pat, somehow inappropriate for the emotion with which it was aimed.

It wasn't fiction, she thought sadly, dismissing all her youthful scribing with a flick of her head, dismissing all her innocent storytelling merely as an escapist illusion, a fabrication, though not a lie, as that somehow seemed too harsh. It wasn't lying, but perhaps bending the truth to allow little additions to creep through the gaps. It wasn't fiction, but merely reality, with a twist. But that was permissible, she thought, as sometimes reality needs that. Sometimes reality needs a little twist.

Once upon a time, there was a woman in a blue suit, who got married to a man in a black suit in a church, on a Saturday afternoon, many years ago, many years after her first wedding, in a white dress, in another life, or so it seemed. Her mother and father were there as well, as was her sister, in an ivory dress this time, with her own husband, who also stood in a similar photo, in a similar frame, on her mother's mantlepiece. The man in a black suit brought his own mother and his own sister, but nobody else. There were no other guests.

Her mother and father and sister were all standing beside her; there was no need for chairs this time, as there weren't enough people to fill them. She had yellow flowers this time and a hat, with no veil. She had pale cream shoes on, with small heels, lent to her by her sister, from her own wedding. She did have white shoes, from the wedding in the white dress, but she didn't want to wear them. How could she? They got married in another church, away from the church of her first wedding and the churchyard where the man in the brown suit was buried, or would have been, had they been given the body.

This church felt cold and empty, with so few people, but she didn't mind. She didn't want this wedding to be the same; she didn't want this marriage to be the same, over before it had begun, surrounded and then overcome by shame and fear. She wanted to begin again and now she had the chance, in this new place, far away from her parents' protection and the whispers of neighbours and friends. She had spent too long at home, too long on her own, sitting in her father's chair, reading books, writing letters and praying for one in

143

return, with Bill the sheepdog sat calmly at her feet, being unfit for anything else, time having worn him down, as with so many other things. She was tired of keeping secrets, keeping quiet, keeping every single emotion under lock and key, never to be touched, never to be found again. She was fed up of hiding from people and their conspiratorial murmurs, their sneaking glances, eyes following her without turning their faces. 'Isn't that the woman whose husband was shot? Terrible thing. I wonder how she can show her face around here. Still, it isn't her fault; can't blame her for marrying him. She couldn't have known what he was like.' She was tired of their shallow suspicions, strangers searching her for any sign that she shared his sympathies. She wanted to scream sometimes, wanted to shout and shriek at them. 'He didn't. He wasn't like that. It was all just a horrible mistake.' But then they wouldn't hear her, they wouldn't accept it. They'd already closed their ears to any arguments long ago. They wouldn't listen to her, even if she tried.

Sally didn't know what to do. Her brain was in a frenzy; ideas, thoughts, images, crossing rapidly to and fro like tangled knitting. Everything her grandmother had said came rushing back to her, every story she'd ever told was rattling away inside her mind, knocking on the sides and screaming to get out.

But it wasn't a story, she reminded herself. It was all true. She shook her head, disbelieving, as she had been for so many years, but unable to do so now. It *was* all true. She had the proof, right there in front of her. She could never have believed it. Never.

She'd backed away long ago from the display case containing that potent letter, aware that the other visitors milling around were staring and sidestepping around her, no doubt noticing her stunned expression and look of dumfounded horror as something different from that of your average tourist. She was walking around now in circles, just walking aimlessly through the empty echoing halls, her shoes making unfortunate clicking noises along marble floors, as her pace quickened and her disorientation increased.

Eventually, she spied a wooden slatted bench and just had to sit down, her mind and emotions overwhelming her. It couldn't be true, it just couldn't. But it was. It was too coincidental. There couldn't be another William Johnson writing to his wife Emma from the trenches, who was killed in 1916. She could hear once more her grandmother's voice floating in her head, she could remember so well the day she told her about him, when Sally, now a fidgety ten years old and no longer so enthralled by her tales as she had been, had wriggled impatiently off the chair beside her, when she began yet another repeat of yesterday's programme.

'I've heard about your wedding before Gran.'

It was then that it happened, just as Sally was scuttling out of the back door, heading for the garden, her grandmother's voice cut through the air, sharply announcing: 'Oh, but I was going to tell you about my other wedding.'

Sally froze in the doorway, aware that her right foot, which was nearly on the path outside, was hovering slightly, having been stopped in mid flight. She turned back to look at her gran, expecting to see her perched on the chair, smiling, as she always was whenever she told Sally anything bordering on the fictitious. But this time she was sitting quite still, sober, solemn, her eyes staring at somewhere or something beyond Sally, looking through her, not at her, as if she wasn't really there at all, but a shadow.

Sally replaced her foot back inside the threshold, curiosity having gripped her and sunk in its teeth, pulling her back to another time, just as her gran knew it would, seizing and snatching at her attention, just when she thought it was slipping away. Sally hesitated before stepping back inside. She was dubious, knowing even at this age that her Gran wasn't entirely truthful when it came to her stories, primarily by the way her mother would stand by and shake her head and accuse her of 'filling the child's mind with nonsense'. But this one... this one was just too tempting and she wanted to know. She stepped back inside, shutting the door sharply, which seemed to bring her gran back to reality, with a snap of her head.

'You had another wedding?' Sally prompted her.

'Oh yes, I was married before your grandfather,' she reported in a brisk, almost matter of fact manner, folding her hands in her lap, her eyes seeing Sally once more, not staring into some infinite abyss where Sally couldn't reach her. She looked immediately more like herself, smiling and cheerful, and Sally felt reassured. She was only pretending. This was just another story, an illusion; nothing more.

Once upon a time, there was a woman in a white dress, who got married to a man in a brown suit, in a church one Saturday many years ago. Her mother and father were there as well, in their Sunday best, even though it was a

Saturday; they made allowances, they had flexibility, in those days. Her sister was there too, in a pale blue dress, decorated by a little hat, with a veil, to make it more appropriate for the occasion. They all wore gloves; the woman and her sister wore white lace, their mother wore black, as she had no other colour to go with her pink suit.

They had a photograph, for the occasion, in a studio down the road from the church. Her mother was sitting down in the photo, with her father standing behind, like the proud, upright head of the family that he was, with his hands folded over each other in front of him and an expression on his face that could best be described as stolid. Smiling, as with colour, was rare in photos. He was wearing a suit, with a waistcoat, tie and pocket watch, which could have been any colour, but was rendered black by the photograph, taken in the time before colour was committed to celluloid.

The woman was wearing a long white dress, with an equally long white veil and a large bouquet of flowers held before her. These could also have been any colour. The man beside her had his arm linked through hers, and was wearing a suit, also with a waistcoat and tie, though not a pocket watch. His suit was brown; a shade not reflected by the photo, but she knew it was brown. She remembered it, even though the image had been held in her mind for many years, and it was probably a little discoloured, a little faded, a little patchy and worn in places, but she still knew it was brown. It was a suit which, in a few months, would be replaced by an army uniform. He was a man who, in a few months, would be killed, in the future which was yet unknown to those in the photograph, where he would only

147

exist in the past, an illusion or a daydream. A man who would be killed, not by the enemy, or some nameless face, but by a man he knew, trusted, even liked. Killed, shot, for failing to obey an officer's order. But all that was yet to come, and that was all it remained, for the moment; an illusion.

But it wasn't, thought Sally, her fingers tearing at the edge of her coat. It did happen, he did exist. He did live. He was killed. It really did happen. She wasn't pretending, she thought regretfully, as whatever illusion she might have thought it was lay shattered, at her feet. Broken pieces that would soon have to be picked up.

INFINITY

It May Be Years

Enid Smith

'Ole Joe' they'd called him for the last twenty years but now he really was 'Ole Joe'. He smiled to himself as he paused on the slope, breathing hard. His body frail and worn from years of toil made hard going of the narrow path to the cliff top.

In the happy days of his youth he'd come running up the path, screaming to frighten the gulls while robbing their nests or to watch for the fishing boats. Then there was Maisie; they'd walked along the cliff top, hand in hand in the cool of a summer evening, the cold biting rain of a stormy winter's day...

He'd had a grand life, by and large, as a fisherman, marrying Maisie and the kiddies growing up. It was sad losing Frank in the war but when you're getting on a bit you take these things in your stride.

A few yards from the edge of the cliff he sat down; there was an old wooden seat where he always sat, looking out to sea. He fumbled in his pocket for his baccy and, having lit his pipe, leaned back with a sigh.

Dear Maisie, they'd had their ups and downs alright and now she was gone. A week ago this very night he'd sat by her bedside, holding her hands, hands wrinkled and knotted like his own. She knew she was dying.

'It won't be long Joe lad, hold me hand. How funny, I'm not afraid,' she whispered and lay back, still and quiet.

Joe leaned forward but her eyes opened and she smiled; 'I'll be waiting for you Joe love, don't be long. God Bless You!'

A little sigh. A flutter of her eyelids and the hands that Joe held became still and lifeless.

He checked back the tears. That was a week ago, he was still here and there was that letter from Ailsa, married to a farmer in Somerset. 'Come and live with us Joe, you're getting old and it may be years yet. You're welcome to all we've got and I know you won't be any trouble. Bring anything with you that you fancy. I've got a room ready for you with a nice bed and a comfy chair, we'll make you at home. You can't live all by yourself in that lonely spot.'

He didn't want to be made at home. His home was here so he'd ignored the letter, then this morning – a telegram, 'Coming to fetch you Saturday. Love Ailsa' – just that. Well, he wasn't going, fight 'em first he would. How could he live away from the sea? Besides when he came up here and sat looking out over the water he could hear Maisie; 'It won't be long love, I'm waiting.'

Ailsa would say he was mad, that she would, but he knew better.

How hazy the sea was when the sun got warm, the little fishing boats swung up and down against the harbour wall. the seagulls screeched and flapped lazily onto the water, up and down they bobbed... up and down. The old man's head nodded, his eyes closed, his pipe fell from his toothless mouth and he slept....

The hot sun beat down on his weather-beaten face, smoothed the deep wrinkles on his brow and under his eyes, warming the frail body and easing his sleep. A butterfly settled on his hat and the sparrows hopped cheekily around him; he was fast asleep.

It was late that afternoon that they found him. Ailsa and her round faced, genial husband. There he was, on the seat, his hands folded, his eyes closed and a smile on his lips.

'Joe, wake up, we've been looking for you everywhere, you haven't packed or anything....' A startled look came over her face, she leaned over and touched his brow, it was still warm from the heat of the sun, she raised his hand, it was cold and lifeless... she put it gently back and turned to her husband.

'Oh Tom!' she cried, 'he's gone!'

Fear of Heights

Llinos Jones

On the highest point of the tallest tower
Elevated above all
You scan this familiar view.
Always beyond reach, now beyond reason
As I cling to unstable battlements
And shield myself from the drop.

Descending, I follow. My feet falter
On concave spiral steps
Worn by violence and legacy
Smoothed to danger
And I develop a new fear
Of depths.

Parting on solid ground, I hold to you
A strange embrace;
Too short to clasp your shoulders,
Or link a circle around your neck
I clinch your waist, lay my head at your
heart,
And hear its beat, strong and steadfast
And it suffices.

Sleep

Lucy Delbridge

Take me to a place where I know I can be
Drifting through my darkening velvet ebony
Show me where the sunset stains the purple sky
Let the sound of silence slowly send us high

I watch the waves of peaceful haze wash over you
Skim the shore of stillness, let it draw you through
You coast along the boulevard of gentle breeze
And journey through the misty blue with ever ease

Sometimes when in paradise, it can open
                                    up the mind
Because, when in sometimes paradise
Everything's alright.

Kite

Llinos Jones

The thinnest cotton
Tethered to my wrist
Is little evidence of you now.
But taut and tugging, a mild bid for freedom
Remains.

Far above
You're a dark diamond cloud,
A distant dancer
Controlled by none but the breeze.
Beyond my reach, of course,
Though somehow bound by
Instinct and the almost imperceptible.

Sometimes this cord sags,
Seems to fall,
Empty
And a slump fills my heart
With visions of frayed endings,
And ragged goodbyes.

Yet you fly again,
Nudging me, tightening the link
Caring little that you
Graze me with your flutter and flurry.

For the binds persist, the ties endure.

La Belle Vue

Jo Perkins

The boy pushed the stone gently with his foot, it scraped dustily against its neighbours, yellow and brown, dry and dead. They were spread out by the side of the road; the men had come the previous spring with their heavy lorries lumbering up the narrow road from the wide valley far below. They built up the sides of the road on its tortuous bends to stop it sliding away down the hillside but now a winter's snow later the stones had leached away from the highway.

The boy bent down and searched for the precise shape of stone that he needed for his building project. His creation was like the houses down on the plain, it had no windows on the outside so that the dust and heat of the summer would be kept out, and enemies. In those houses, the windows looked in onto a central courtyard which funnelled up the breeze and the smoke from the cooking fires. Unlike his house, whose windows gazed out onto the vast flat bottomed valley stretching away to the next range of mountains blue on the horizon. His house took its name from that, Belle Vue, the passing French had named it. It was a staging post at a sharp bend on the high mountain pass offering rooms and food to travellers who passed its door, more than two and a half thousand metres above the sea.

It was quiet: heavy snow over the last few days had caused the trickle of vehicles to dwindle. The boy looked behind him towards the tiny restaurant, he saw his father and two other men inside drinking mint tea, huddled in their djellabahs. Khalid must be there somewhere as well, his car had been left carelessly outside. He had a shop for tourists down on the plain but he preferred to bring his bag of Tuareg silver up to the Belle Vue where the romance of the altitude brought him higher prices. Behind the restaurant the highest peaks were still thick with snow against the blue January sky; their lower slopes on this side were warmed by the sun, but on the other side of the mountain, out of the sun's rays, the snow would linger.

The boy turned back to the valley. He looked down at the road winding far below and changed it in his mind into his mother's ball of thread that would fall to the floor without permission and roll and unwind under the chairs on the hard marble floor. He pulled the road of thread, unsnaking it from the brown mountain side, twitching it out from behind the corner where he knew it ran out of sight, its repetitive bends a faint line against the dry scrubby hillsides with their smooth folds. He pulled again and the road, now almost invisible to his sharp young eye, jerked down hundreds of metres into the nearest narrow valley where patches of green nestled near the dry river bottom and the square buildings huddled with their windows looking inwards. He saw the shining roof of the new school next to the mosque. His brothers would be there now. He should be there now but his mother sensing his anguish that morning had taken pity on him. He closed his eyes to make the school disappear; through the bright sun on his closed eyelids he heard the asthmatic wheeze of a donkey far below and smelled the faint whiff of fire as a farmer burnt off some of the hillside to scrape a bit more of a living from the arid land. He opened his eyes again; unfortunately the school was still there. Beyond the village the road he could no longer see led down to the wide fertile plain. Its manmade tomato houses gleamed faraway in the sun and puffs of sand and smoke blew hazily into the distance across the big towns, on to the next mountains and the Sahara beyond.

Something nearer caught his eye: down in the cleft between the scabby mountainsides, flickers of white lazily floated and drifted like plastic bags caught in a breeze. From this distance they moved at a pace so leisurely they should have fallen from the air. They circled upwards a reverse vortex, eddying and swaying, sometimes sinking behind a rocky outcrop and back into sight again. The storks were back. Thirty or forty of them. They basked on the thermal currents from the hot valley, swirling and drifting up over the high mountains, down into the valley beyond and the fish filled river swollen with snow melt

'Say... eed, Say... eed', he heard his mother calling. He saw her behind the buildings, her hand shielding her eyes as she searched for her son. The blue of her scarf a colour

160

so intense that it seemed she must have reached up to the midnight sky and pulled down a stretch of deep blue to veil herself against men she did not know. Sayeed looked down reluctantly at his building efforts. He would have to come back later and design the roof. He leapt up and as he turned round to run across the road to the restaurant his foot caught the corner of his half built palace and dislodged a stone which tumbled away, bouncing free and fast down the loose shale of the hillside.

The stone came from nowhere. Bouncing down the hillside, it skimmed and hit the windscreen, crazing and splintering the glass. The driver braked sharply, the back wheels slipped on the loose stones and slid unpleasantly close to the edge before the front of the car hit the mountainside and lodged there, skewed sideways across the road, its nose embedded in the dark yellow earth.

'Jeez, what was that?'

The large American woman in the backseat unravelled herself from her seatbelt and wrenched the car door open. Her companion, stunned into silence by the shock of finding herself still alive, half fell out after her.

'Christ!... Look at Mohammed!'

She pulled open the passenger door with the strength that she normally reserved for securing herself a place at the front of a queue.

The driver, Mohammed, was slumped sideways, his face grey with a trickle of blood edgeing down his face.

'Wake up! Wake up,' she shouted.

'Eleanor you gotta do something. Haven't you done first aid?'

Eleanor was quite in need of first aid herself at this point. Mostly the sort of first aid that came in a brandy bottle and was unlikely to be found high up on a mountain pass in an Islamic country. Nevertheless she remembered her pioneer forebears, looked over the precipice which had nearly caused her to join her long dead relations, dusted her hands and took a look inside the car.

Mohammed's face had a unhealthy tinge but his eyes opened and he focused on the determined face of the short grey haired woman who was trying to work out if he was still alive.

'I'm so sorry Mrs Bennington, I'm so sorry,' his eyes closed again.

'It wasn't your fault Mohammed, you were wonderful, we could have gone straight over the edge, you saved us. Where are you injured?'

'It's my leg, Mrs Bennington, my leg.'

The redoubtable Eleanor Bennington, twice divorced but fortunately with enough of an inheritance to keep her nicely in foreign travel, peered down into the footwell of the driver's seat. Mohammed's leg did indeed seem to be at an unusual angle. The car door had been pushed in against it by the impact of the crash.

'We must get him out of the car, Eleanor, it may catch fire or some thing may come right round this corner straight into us.' Eleanor's companion wobbled about agitatedly..

Eleanor appraised the problem, and tried to think what her first husband, Mort, would have done in the circumstances. She couldn't ever remember him doing anything decisive, which was why she had divorced him. So she was forced to rely on her own feminine instincts which usually proved effective.

The driver's door was stove in, there did not appear to be a human being for many miles, if not several centuries, and they had a good looking young man incapacitated with possibly serious injuries.

'Can you move your leg?' she asked.

Mohammed winced but managed to move his leg a few inches.

'If you lean over into the passenger seat, Peggy and I will try and pull you out. I'm afraid it may hurt.'

Eleanor reached under Mohammed's armpits with her birdlike arms and tugged, futilely.

Peggy pushed her out of the way, grasped the injured driver and with one yank he was outside the car like a recalcitrant molar. Lying in the road and groaning in agony.

The two American ladies stood back and wondered what to do. Having solved one problem they now faced a catalogue of new ones.

The chances of a passing helicopter spotting them were pretty remote, there was no signal for mobile phones.

'Mohammed, where do we go to find help?'

'You must make the car horn sound... they will hear it... at the Belle Vue.'

He shut his eyes with the pain.

The ladies exchanged bemused looks. There were obviously no houses for miles, the man was rambling. But what else could they do?

Eleanor wriggled back inside, located the horn symbol and pressed.

Some five hundred metres above them four figures appeared.

Jean Claude took his eyes away from the road briefly to look at his watch. He had been driving for more than six hours and the road continued to loop relentlessly through the mountains. His shirt sleeve still with its politely ironed crease slid smoothly back over the casing of his watch. His mind went back to the telephone conversation with his partner before he left the city, how much his reputation would depend on this new venture. The market for riads in the city was drying up, the families who owned the ancient traditional buildings in the kasbah knew exactly how much they could extract for them from the foreign buyers. There were no longer the bargains to be had from old people just glad to sell off their family homes in the old quarter and move into modern appartments with running water and kitchens. But the demand for luxury holidays was growing and not just for holidays; more and more French people wanted to own their own properties in this their old colony. Jean Claude's skills as an architect had been much in demand, but he was now having to look further afield. His partner had needed to stay in their minimalist tiny office in France overseeing the interior designs for their last project. They had spent months working on it, a three storey twisted mediaeval building which would welcome high spending French couples with its plasma screens and organdie curtains wafting gently in the breeze that no longer smelled of drains and ancient misdemeanours.

Jean Claude was now out hunting, looking for more

neglected buildings that he could lovingly sculpt into homes fit for refugees from the leaden skies of Northern Europe, but it was taking a long time, too long. The hours spent on the dusty road that had been forced through the mountains by his predecessors in the 1930s should have been hours spent planning bathrooms, measuring courtyards and balconies. He was going to investigate an ancient walled town further south. The road had been worse than he had expected, its surface nibbled away by the winter's frost and snow. He'd chosen this route from the city because he wanted to take photos for his new brochure. They would soon be printed most economically at a small family press here and despatched to the lounges and the salons of the motherland. But Jean Claude had stopped too long to admire and photograph the strange geological palette of the high rolling peaks. The icy shade on the north facing side of the mountains was spreading and the blue of the sky was deepening. Just a few more kilometres and he would be over the highest part of the pass and down into the plain, back to the land of restaurants, clean towels and bidets.

The sun in front of him shifted south now south west but then flickered and blotched. Jean Claude ducked involuntarily then braked sharply as the sky in front of his car turned against him. Missiles surged out from a gap in the rocks. He pulled the car over to the side of the road where the snow still clung, pushed up his sunglasses and watched as the missiles spread their huge black ragged wings, elongated their white necks and pointed their beaks down to the valley. Thirty or forty enormous storks cruised overhead. Jean Claude reached for his camera but the birds banked quickly and their prehistoric forms slipped out of sight.

He started the car again, his heart still beating a little bit too quickly. The road looped its last loop and curled through a slice in the rock; before him the broad plain on the other side of the mountains rolled away into the distance. A delapidated restaurant hugged one side of the road; on the other, small rocks littered the frayed edge of the tarmac which dissolved into a sheer drop.

A man lurched into the road, gesticulating at him. For the second time in a few minutes Jean Claude's foot hit the brake hard. He slithered to a stop on the loose surface of the road.

'Monsieur, monsieur, you cannot go any further, the road is blocked.'

Jean Claude looked impatiently at the man, the building behind him and the wide valley with the town, now tantalisingly close.

'A car has met with an accident and is blocking the road. We are waiting for a truck to come and pull it out of the way. You are welcome to wait in our restaurant, here at the Belle Vue.'

There was no sign of any accident but if it was a ploy to lure customers into his establishment Jean Claude had to admire the man's cheek. He reluctantly turned his car off the road into the small car park, squeezing past a badly parked ancient Mercedes. Two elderly women tourists sat on the restaurant's modest terrace, built to make the most of the amazing view. He carefully locked the car door and went into the restaurant, unhappy at the prospect of being forced to waste precious time in this rocky outpost.

'Saalamoo aleekom,' Jean Claude greeted the man hovering inside the door.

'Waalykom salam,' the man replied, may peace be upon you too.

A small boy stood in a dark corner behind the counter, immersed in the shadows, moving nothing except his eyes.

Sayeed watched his father carrying more bottles of soft drinks out to the American ladies sitting on the terrace, their bags strewn about in the sun. The sudden influx of visitors had lifted the gloom that lurked about the place on these winter's days. Warm spicy smells drifted out from the small kitchen and Sayeed heard his mother scraping pots and the hiss and spit of hot oil. There were frequent accidents on the narrow winding mountain road, many of them with tragic consequences. But the American ladies had been so grateful when Sayeed's father and his friends helped them the few hundred yards up to the restaurant at the Belle Vue. They insisted on paying for their food even though his father said there was no need. As a consequence he only added another fifty per cent to their bill instead of doubling it. The smaller one had tried to make a fuss of Sayeed but he had panicked and ducked under his father's arm and run free into the kitchen to his mother. A car from the village below had taken their driver to hospital but the ladies had to wait for the road to be unblocked and another taxi to take them over the mountain pass.

Sayeed dawdled behind the counter, curious at the unexpected activity but at the same time uneasy with the strangers. The whine of an over-stretched engine carried up

167

from the mountainside below, followed by the sound of metal sliding over rock. The man, who had complained about his coffee, sat at one of the inside tables. His car had French number plates. He had a computer. Sayeed had seen them in the shop with glass windows on the road to the bus station in the town. The man's fingers fidgeted at the keyboard, he glanced up at the windows, the walls, the windows again. Sayeed could see lines and boxes on the computer screen.

He wondered why the foreigner was sitting inside. The light inside was dim even when the bare electric bulbs were lit, swinging on their wires high among the insects. The bare concrete walls had been painted once, but Sayeed's father said there was no point in painting them again as the foreign tourists always sat outside. It was only the locals, with no need to admire the view, who sat here warm between the thick walls in winter and out of the heat in summer. Entranced, Sayeed sidled out from his shadows to see the patterns that the Frenchman was making on his screen; he watched as windows and staircases sprang out of nowhere and hung delicately in the air, one tap and then they all disappeared, instead the form of another building emerged in lines. Familiar lines which matched those of his own house. Sayeed saw the man making holes in the walls, his walls, his windows, that looked outwards onto the great plain. The man measured the room behind him with his eyes and tapped again at his keyboard.

Sayeed slid back behind the refrigerated drinks but not quickly enough. The Frenchman clicked his fingers and called out to him in bad Arabic, 'Boy! Ask your father when the road will be open.'

Sayeed turned, pretending he had not understood, but his father was already there behind him.

'Not long, monsieur, not long.'

The man pulled a face and went back to his laptop. Moments later the angry grating sound which had been grumbling out of sight became suddenly louder and a rusty yellow lorry came into view dragging a reluctant taxi by its front bumper.

The Frenchman looked up startled, then relieved as he realised the obstruction had been removed from the road. He leapt up, zipped his laptop into its black leather case and rushed out of the room, flinging a handful of coins on the counter. He pulled the door handle on his car, forgetting he'd locked it, then set his laptop case on the car roof while he emptied his pockets impatiently looking for his car keys. In his haste they fell to the floor. Cursing, he picked them up from among the loose stones which threatened to swallow them up. Inside the car at last, he threw it into gear and drove off with a rattle of flying stones. The car rounded the bend slightly too fast, throwing up a cloud of dust, and headed downhill and away, the engine noise suddenly muffled behind the rocky cliff below.

Sayeed's father, all smiles, after having just pocketed an excessive tip, escorted the two American ladies to their new taxi. Sayeed trailing silently behind him like a wisp of smoke.

'Thank you so much,' said his father, as he lifted their bags into the boot. 'I hope you enjoy the rest of your journey.'

The larger of the two American ladies fumbled in her bag and produced something which she gave to Sayeed.

The boy looked at the object in his hand. It was a pen

with two circular black ears at the end and a face. The face of a cartoon mouse. He almost smiled at her.

She turned to her smaller companion.

'Come on Eleanor, we must leave this gorgeous place, the driver wants to go.'

Eleanor tucked the silver necklace that she had just bought for her niece into a side pocket of her rather sensible bag, and trotted round to the other side of the car. It sped off, the travellers waving enthusiastically as it rounded the bend.

Sayeed helped his father clear the tables, wiping away the sticky rings. The silence was broken by clinks of metal as Khalid sat inside wrapping his unsold silver carefully in cloths. Sayeed went outside, the cold air creeping fast as the sun slipped down deep orange into the smoke of the horizon, draining the colour from the land. The damaged taxi had been left skewed across the side of the road just leaving enough room for vehicles to pass. Sayeed would have time now to finish building his house before the light went altogether.

He searched the roadside and found that despite the chaos of the last couple of hours the four walls of his miniature house remained unscathed. He bent down to replace a missing corner stone that had come adrift and looked around the rapidly darkening hillside for something to make a roof. Hanging over the edge of the sharp drop was a black rectangular shape that he had not noticed before. Sayeed went to investigate. It was the bag containing the Frenchman's computer. He wondered if he should take it inside to his father but quickly rejected that idea as he had not liked the Frenchman and it was exactly

the right size for a roof for his house. He placed it respect-
fully on top of the four walls and put a stone at each corner
of the black oblong to make a pleasingly symmetrical shape.
He paused to admire his work, then picked up some smaller
stones to make a border around the edge of his new roof
terrace. The soft dark mountain night made it almost
impossible to see now but as an afterthought, he piled on
more stones, covering the bag completely. It became part of
the hillside, just another rocky mound in a very rocky place.
It would be safe there until the Frenchman came back; they
always came back.

Before

Lucy Delbridge

Crimson thoughts meander gently
Liquid turns to rust
Stagnant pools evaporate
As images combust
Shards of reason pierce softly
Through my opening mind
Consciousness releases slowly
Leaving me behind
Distant pain still reaches for me
Wandering round my head
Reaching and entwining me
Leaving me for dead
Now I'm falling
Now I'm writhing
Fate rips out my heart
Callous knives and spikes of hatred
Tearing me apart

Too late now
I'm gone
I'm going
I'll see you soon no doubt
I'll leave you to your lifeless living
I know I got out

Come and Stand in the Rain with Me

Jessie Ledbetter

The call came in the middle of the night. His hand groped towards the phone on the nightstand and his wife muttered in her sleep before rolling away from him and the shrill ring. 'Noah? Honey, it's your mother. Lillie's missing again and I've got my curlers in, not to mention the Subaru's still down at Joe's Mechanics and won't be ready till Friday.'

'Okay Mom. I'm getting up; I'll find her.'

He hung up the phone and his wife Jane looked over her shoulder at him. 'Your mother again? Isn't there anyone else she can call?'

It was useless to argue. 'No, Jane, it's three in the morning. There's no one else.'

His Jeep was cold and he drove hunched over the steering wheel. He'd fiddled with the heat but it only sputtered, yet another thing to fix. He thought about cranking up the radio to counteract the quiet but couldn't find the energy to turn the knob.

He drove through the neighbourhoods surrounding his mother's house, the soft patter of the rain hitting the roof of the Jeep the only sound in the night. He stuck his hand out, felt the water drip down his arm and into his shirt. It was brutally cold but smelled of spring.

He found her on the corner of Front and Park St, standing with her head thrown back, her nightdress plastered to her skin, her toes bare and curled in against the cold of the cement. Her hair fell down her back in one black tangled glob and her eyes were shut, the rain running down her face.

He pulled over, left the engine running. He hunched into his coat, the sweet smelling rain more of a nuisance now that it was running down his collar and not just his arm.

'Lillie!' he hollered.

'Hi Noah.'

'Come on, it's time to go home.'

'It smells so good.'

'I know. Come on, you're going to get sick.'

'It'll be worth it.'

'Mom's worried. That's why she called me.'

Lillie took a deep breath, filling her lungs with air. 'Mom's always worried. I'm a grown up now.'

'I know Lillie. Come on, into the car.'

'Why don't you ever stand in the rain with me anymore, Noah?'

'Because Lillie. It's cold. Hurry up now.'

'It's soft. On your cheeks.' She pressed her fingers into her skin, leaving five red marks on either side of her face.

'Lillie.' Noah was now thoroughly wet. 'Come on.' He took her arm, led her to the car.

The ride back to his mother's house was quiet. Lillie fell asleep with her head bobbing against the window, a soft thud, thud, thud whenever he went around a corner.

Their mother Ruth was waiting up in the living room. Her grey hair was tightly wound in curlers and her bathrobe was the same hunter green one his father had given her on their last Christmas together. It was frayed and ragged now and he could see the stitching where she'd tried to mend it. 'Oh thank goodness, I got so worried, Noah, so very worried when I found her missing. I mean, really, if I hadn't gotten up to get my tea who knows what would have happened!' She rushed her words together, trying to fit more into the silence between them than needed to be said. Her teeth were crooked and yellow with age and when she smiled at him Noah had to force himself not to focus on them.

'I know Mom. I have to go home now. I'll stop by later today.'

She kept smiling at him, the smile of the old and slightly senile, resting her hand on his arm. Her nails were painted the faintest of pinks but it was the blue and green veins that seemed like spider webs across the back of her hand that Noah found most disconcerting. That, and the overpowering scent of lavender. Ruth would turn seventy in a few months.

It was too early in the morning, or too late in the night, to think about it now. Noah turned and left, pulling the front door closed behind him.

Noah's parents moved their family to Farmington, Maine to get them out of the city. Ruth always said they moved because of the quiet; the quiet and the rain. There was a moment from Noah's childhood, one that he remembered more than any other, where he stood on the lawn of their new two-storey farmhouse that sat a mile off the road in a small clearing amidst a forest of trees, looking at the peeling paint with disgust, wishing to return to Boston where at least the streets housed people and not only trees. His kid sister Lillie had come running, her arms flung out wide and her eyes closed, the happiest look he'd ever seen on a person's face plastered across hers. 'It's going to rain, it's going to rain!' she grinned at him but Noah didn't smile back, and their father Allen stopped unloading the back of the station wagon to watch.

But now Allen was dead and Farmington had lost its idealistic state years ago. Noah stayed for Lillie and he and everyone around him knew it. Jane was coming to resent him for it and the thought, which should have left fear swirling up his throat, brought only weariness.

Jane was awake and very angry when he got home. 'Did you find her?'

'I found her.'

'This is the second time this month.'

'Yes I know.'

Noah, this is getting ridiculous.'

'Yes, it is.'

'She can't keep letting Lillie out like that. She's going to get lost, or hurt.'

'Yep.'

'Noah, I'm serious. You have to talk to her.'

'Okay.'

Jane arched a brow, always perfectly cropped, behind the solid tiger-striped rim of her glasses and pinched her lips together, though her lips were too wide and too plump for the effect to work. 'Are you even listening to me?'

Noah sighed. 'Not now, Jane. I'm going to bed.'

'What about your novel?' she asked but Noah ignored her and retreated into the bedroom.

He lay down on the mattress in the quiet and tried to fall back asleep. He could hear Jane clicking the heel of her shoe on the blue linoleum in the kitchen. They'd meant to replace it. When they'd bought the house they'd spent nights giggling together, planning their renovations on the nineteen seventies disaster they'd just bought. But then Taylor had been born, Allen had his first stroke and Ruth began to have panic attacks. Before Noah had time to breathe, Allen was dead, Ruth was turning seventy and the prospect of what would happen to Lillie became all too real.

Noah heard Jane muttering to herself as she left the house and pulled the door shut behind her with a definitive thud.

Noah kept his word to his mother and after he picked Taylor up from school, they headed over to his mother's. He brought a bag of groceries, set it on the counter as Ruth fawned over Taylor's latest drawing of the dog he so desperately wanted. 'Oh Taylor baby, that sure is one pretty dog.'

Taylor raised a brow, a move so ideally Jane that Noah coughed. 'Can I have one Dad? Please? I'd take real good care of it, really I would.'

'Maybe Taylor,' Noah said, running his hand over his son's soft head. Barely old enough for school, he thought, not yet old enough for a dog.

'Where's Aunt Lillie? She said we could play on the swing set next time I came over.' Taylor looked at his grandmother with expectant eyes and Ruth smiled in a way that Noah could only describe as smiling through him for Ruth was already somewhere else. Noah opened his mouth to take over the conversation, to avoid the confusion and hurt Taylor was bound to feel when Ruth unconsciously ignored him, but then Lillie appeared and with a giggle, took Taylor into the backyard to play.

Ruth shook herself and set to it happily, unpacking the groceries and cutting the carrots over the sink. 'They're so good together, Lillie just adores Taylor and when he comes over, she's so happy. She misses having someone to play with her. You two used to invent the most amazing games; always running around underfoot. It's so quiet now.'

Noah sensed it coming. 'Mom, It's been over a year. Lillie's gotten over Dad's death.'

Ruth only smiled, faintly, and ran the tomatoes under the water from the sink. 'Of course she has, dear, of course she has.' They sat in silence for a while, Noah pursuing the headlines of the paper, Ruth finishing with the vegetables. The quiet was becoming too intense for Ruth. 'What do you think you will do? With her, I mean.'

'Do with her what Mom?'

Ruth made a little clicking noise at the side of her mouth. The skin that had once ridden high on her cheekbones converged there by the side of her mouth and gave her the appearance of looking in a funny mirror. 'When I'm gone of course. I'll be 70 in a few months, Noah Mathew.'

'I know, Mom.'

'So what are your plans for your sister when I'm gone?' Ruth dried her hands on the kitchen towel then sat across from Noah at the table. She blinked three times rapidly and smiled as if she thought it would ease some of the tension. 'I won't be able to care for her much longer. Will you put her in a home?'

Noah didn't want to have this conversation, not now when he was lacking sleep and certainly not again. They'd been having some version of what he'd come to consider the 'Lillie Chat' every few weeks since his father had died a year ago. And as Ruth's birthday approached and her thoughts turned more to her own impending departure, they'd been having a 'Lillie Chat' every few days. These chats never ended well and no matter what Noah said or did, Ruth was never satisfied with his response. Disgusted with the whole idea, Noah stood. 'I'll come back for Taylor later, Mom.' Not at all sure where he was going, Noah left.

Almost a week and a half went by before Noah was again awakened by his mother. April was turning out to be a rainy month and Noah was beginning to feel as if the skies were conniving against him as well. 'Honey, I'm so sorry, I know what a burden this is for you but I just don't trust that Subaru, you know I think Joe is conning me, maybe you should take it in next week for me. Will you go and find her? Bring her home and I promise, I'll find some way to keep her in the house.'

Noah hung up without a word and climbed out of bed.

He found her standing in front of the library, tapping her fingers on the stone sign outside. She turned when he pulled up, the face of a seasoned woman but the heart and

179

mind of a child. She grinned, sticking her tongue between her teeth, and hopped up to sit on the wall.

'Lillie,' Noah said, 'you've got to stop going out in the middle of the night.'

'But it's so pretty at night. Nobody's moving, all the animals are sleeping. It's quiet.'

'Yes, Lillie. That's what night time is for.'

'Why don't we come here any more? Do they still have story time?' Lillie looked at the red-stone building, the walk-way leading to three short steps and a wide wooden door.

'Because I went away to school; Emerson College? In Boston?' Noah took a step closer. 'Remember?'

'I know you went back to Boston, where we lived before we lived here.' Lillie hopped off the wall, laid down in the grass. 'Dad was still alive then.'

Feeling unsafe in this territory, Noah sat on the wall. 'Yes. Yes, he was alive then.'

'We all drove down, in the old red car.' Lillie rolled over, and over again, until the jeans and formless yellow sweater were wet with the morning dew. 'You had so many boxes. I carried your suitcase. All the way up.' She moved her fingers, climbing the invisible stairs. 'Three storeys, 46 steps.'

'Yes.' Noah started twitching his foot. 'I thought you were okay with Dad being gone.'

'Oh I am.' Lillie sat up, crossed her legs under her. 'We talked. Mom and me, you and me, Mom and you and me. I know Dad's in a good place. I hope it rains there.' Lillie closed her eyes and smiled.

'Yes, Lillie, I hope it rains there too.'

'Remember when we were little? So small we fit into

Taylor's shoes. He he, you would look so funny in Taylor's shoes.' She opened one eye. 'Red is not your colour, Noah.'

'Thank you.'

'We'd stand in the rain. Let it slide down our cheeks, into our hair, dance on our tongues.' Lillie held her tongue out now as if willing the sky to rain. 'Do you remember, Noah? Mom used to get so mad but we'd just stand and stand, all day long.'

'Yeah, Lillie, I remember.'

'Dad was alive then too.'

'Yes, Dad was alive then too.'

Noah sat in his office later, the cursor on his computer blinking, but he couldn't write. He couldn't seem to push Lillie out of his mind. She was everything good should be and yet her innocence brought the most astounding conflict. He tossed the stress ball Taylor had made him in art class back and forth and stared at the page number on the clean page of his word document: 46. Hadn't Lillie said there'd been 46 steps in his dorm? She'd remember something like that, he mused. Lillie was a master of detail; she knew just when the flowers in the meadow behind their old house would bloom and she'd remember all the colours so she could tell Taylor about them.

Taylor. He was another person to throw into the equation. Was it fair to force Taylor to have to become an adult while his favourite playmate remained a child? Noah could see no alternative but he knew from the arguments and avoided conversations he and Jane had been having for the past year, a different batch of 'Lillie Chats', that Jane thought it disgusting, unjust – Taylor was their child, Lillie was just his sister.

Could he really think that though? Noah clicked out of the Word document that held the beginnings of his fourth novel and leaned back in the chair. It was raining again and Noah had no doubt Lillie was somewhere in it. It was pounding down, a sleek grey blur against the glass, the sound of millions of tiny shards of glass hitting brick. Could he really consider Lillie just his sister? Wasn't she in some way his child too? She was his to protect and love just as much as Taylor. But would Jane force him to choose? And what of Ruth? Would she finally demand an ultimatum? Would he have to confront Jane?

Wearied, Noah left the office, the sound of the rain against the house following him from the room.

Jane came home early from work a few nights later. She tossed her briefcase and suit jacket over the couch and kicked her heels off by the door, something she never did for fear that Taylor would put something inside them. But Taylor was in his room, making all kinds of racket, when she looked up and caught Noah's eye through the door into his office. Noah gritted his teeth before she even spoke. 'We have to talk.'

And he knew, in that moment, that she would force him to choose. 'Fine.' He closed out of Word, saved the draft. He'd only made it to page 48 anyway. Then he crossed his arms over his chest, knowing it would piss her off but too tired to care.

Jane reached up and pulled off her hose, not wanting to get a run and ruin them, before walking in and sitting down on the edge of his desk. 'I don't want to do this any more.'

'Do what exactly?'

'This. This not talking thing.'

'You said we needed to talk. I'm listening.'

'We do need to talk Noah.' She looked at him for a long moment, seeming to study his eyes as if she hadn't seen them in a long while. 'This is more than Lillie.'

Noah shifted, uncomfortable. Jane had a tendency to go straight to the bulk of the matter. 'Lillie's most of it, I'd wager.'

Jane smiled but it didn't reach far. 'Stop it. Stop avoiding it.'

'I'm not avoiding anything, Jane.'

She bit down on her lip and shook her head. 'You've been avoiding it for months. And I've let you too.' She leaned back and crossed her arms.

The quiet started to build so Noah opened his mouth. 'What are you trying to get at here, Jane? Because you say it's not about Lillie but I don't know what else it could be about.'

'Don't get defensive. I'm not attacking Lillie.' Jane stood, her own temper flaring now. 'Lillie isn't a problem; it's you.'

Noah raised his brows. 'Me? Now I'm at fault?'

'Yeah, Noah, you're at fault. All you do is sit here and write, but you don't really write you just pretend to write. You're a balding, pudgy man stuck in middle age with a sister he doesn't know what to do with, a life he doesn't want and two books that sold in only half a dozen bookstores. What have you made of yourself, hm?'

Noah smiled condescendingly, knowing that Jane would hate it. 'This is it, this right here is your problem with me, with Lillie, with my family. You think I haven't made something of myself, is that it? Because you've done so much better, eh, Jane? Working for an insurance company, putting in 40 hours a week with a time clock and a scheduled 30 minute lunch? Is that the key to a fulfilling life? Do you feel fulfilled, Jane?'

Jane stepped forward and her hand flew across his cheek. 'Don't you dare make fun of me, Noah. You think that because I didn't go to college, I'm not as smart as you. Well you're just as stupid, Noah, just as lame and backwards. You've kept yourself, and us, here in Maine where life is so slow and pointless that we all fall asleep even thinking about it.'

The room fell into an uneasy silence. 'Don't ever hit me again,' Noah said.

Jane shook her head, backing towards the door. She stood in the frame, simply staring at him. Then she said, 'I knew you wouldn't choose me.'

Two weeks later, the phone rang again, Ruth's chipper voice on the other end. Noah didn't even answer; he hung up, tossing the phone across the room. It hit the TV, made a loud cracking noise. Not that there was anyone to hear it; Jane had left for New York three days ago and Taylor was spending the night at a friend's. Noah groped in the dark for his pants.

'Lillie,' Noah growled when he found her standing in front of their old house over on Lake Ave. She sat on the old tyre swing, surely unsafe now since the rope hadn't been replaced since Noah was a teenager, gazing ahead of her at the woods. She wore a skirt tonight, one of the brown concoctions she'd find at the Wal-Mart down the highway on the way to Portland. She wore her snow boots with it, bright purple Uggs that must have easily weighed ten pounds per foot. She had one of the old ski hats with the rainbow stripes pulled down almost to her eyes and her hair fell in a haphazard braid down her back. 'Lillie, come on, I don't have time for this,' Noah said.

'We have all the time in the world,' Lillie whispered. 'All we have is time. Lots and lots of time.' She kicked her feet, set the swing moving.

Noah could hear the first stirrings of life there in the woods, the first chirpings of birds. The sun wasn't up yet but they knew, as nature had taught them, that it was just over the horizon.

Lillie twisted so that she was swinging, facing Noah. 'Where's Taylor? And why don't you call any more?'

'Lillie, enough's enough. You're a big enough girl, a woman now, and you understand it's wrong to go walking alone at night.'

Lillie frowned. 'It's going to rain.'

Noah looked up. The clouds did look heavy. 'Lillie, it will always rain. For the rest of your life, it will always rain. You don't have to be in it every time.'

'Will you stand in the rain with me, Noah?'

Noah sighed. 'Lillie. I have to go home.'

Lillie raised a brow, a look that made her look her 32 years. 'Am I problem, Noah? For you, for Mom? Not me, Lillie, a problem, but is my problem a problem?'

'No, Lillie. You're not a problem. You're problem isn't a problem.'

'I don't want to be a problem. I want to live with you someday. And Taylor. Taylor wants me to live with him too.'

'You will, Lillie, you will.'

'Stand in the rain with me, Noah. Like when we were

185

kids. Like when Dad was alive.' She climbed off the swing, moved out into the yard. She was silent for a while, simply looking up at the sky. Then she turned and looked him straight in the eye. 'It was easier when Dad was alive. When Dad was alive, I didn't need to stand in the rain as often.'

'Why do you need to now?'

'Because he's in it. In the rain, I mean.' Lillie took a deep breath. 'It's coming.' And sure enough, within moments, the skies opened up and the rain fell down in gentle splats against the ground. 'You and me, Noah,' Lillie said with a giggle. 'It'll always be you and me.'

'Yes, Lillie, it will always be you and me.'

'Stand with me in the rain, Noah. Come and stand with me.' She came over, pulled on his hand. Noah let himself be led out from under the tree and into the water. 'Turn your face towards it,' Lillie whispered, linking fingers. She closed her eyes and the smile on her face was the largest he'd ever seen.

Noah turned his face up to the sky and let the rain fall down on him.

Black Friday

Llinos Jones

A lupine moon is brimming over Carmarthen
blurring her boundaries again,
bleaching the streets with her beams
but you are far
and I cannot tell you
how the lights hang frozen over
Lammas Street, and all is silent
save for
the chinking echo of stilettos
on hard fresh frost.
I cannot tell of
revellers rolling from the The Gold
roaring in the stillness of the hoary light
and pairing into shadows
of deepset doorways for frozen stolen kisses,
for you are not here.
Bedraggled tinsel strews the street,
thumped beats ricochet through the bars,
glittered gaudiness abounds in icy drunken reels
but I cannot tell you
for you are far.

Life Less Colourful

Lucy Delbridge

I open my eyes and look up directly towards the sky, it's still the same summer's day it was when they last closed, but now I am on the ground. My eyes have been closed for some time, they feel sticky and heavy. Although I know I have not been asleep, I don't actually know where I have been.

My body has an interesting numbness, a kind of fairytale feeling where everything is slightly out of focus, but still kind of garish and bright. Fairies clad in flowing satin dance across the lawn, a misty feeling glides around my head and tiny needles pierce imaginary holes in every pore in my skin. It is not an altogether unpleasant feeling, just unnerving. The mist disperses slowly, so I try to move, try to get the hollow feeling to pass, it won't. The numbness makes everything seem overly heavy; my body seems to be absorbing the ground itself, sinking into the dusty floor.

There is something missing, something that I have not yet noticed. It is something important, vital to the picture, why can't I see it? I know it's not there, but all I can focus on seems to be staring right back at me, I can see the green grass fingers caressing the sides of the garden path with their feather – like touch, I can see the vibrant yellow of the dandelion heads bobbing to the rhythm of the bumble bee's wing dance as he presents his solo recital of an age old performance. I can even make out the shape and colour of the kitchen door, letter box red, it outshines the rest of the house, leaving it looking drab. Painting the side of that house is a job for this forthcoming summer I think. Paint, I can smell paint, or something chemical like that. I breathe in the toxic fumes momentarily dizzying myself; it is a refreshing way to clear my head of all the fog, but it only replaces it with a slightly nauseating haze. I drift, still unable to make out what it is that I have lost, it is something vital, if I could only remember...

Somebody is running towards me, it's my daughter, so I try to get up, she can't see me lying like this on the ground, she'll think that there is something wrong. My body is still glued to the soil, I can merely twitch and shudder which is probably more frightening looking than not moving at all, so I stop. She drops down beside me, 'Mum! Mum what's wrong? What's happened? Can you hear me Mum... Mum?' A look of unmistakable dread overwhelms her delicate face, 'I'm fine,' I say, 'There is nothing wrong, don't worry pet.' But she does not seem to hear me; did the words leave my mouth? Her eyes well up with fresh salt water, her beautiful eyes, blue like Indian oceans, but... wait, I don't see it, that's what is missing, that's what I can't see, it's blue, the colour blue. Where is the blue? The sky, the flaky paint on the side of the house, there is no blue... it's gone.

Reaching for her mobile phone she calls an ambulance, she thinks I'm going to die. In her eyes I see nothing but the teardrops that cascade down her face like rain on a window pane. There is still no blue. I wish she could hear me, 'Don't panic love, I need you to stay calm.' What's that? I can hear a curious droning noise, like a lawn mower chewing up plastic or a motorbike revving its engine. It is a few minutes before I realise that the noise is coming from me, it's the sound my words are making, like I'm speaking through toffee. 'Don't try to speak Mum, save your energy. It's not long before the ambulance comes, I've rung Dad, and he'll meet us at the hospital. It's going to be OK Mum... I love you.' Her voice echoes in the chasm I can't escape from. I am on my own in here.

The paramedics arrive in their olive green uniforms, they call out my name but I feel too tired to answer. They calm my distraught daughter and whisk me into their healing lair; they speak in caring tones and smell of latex and newness. The vivid tangerine orange of the interior dazzles me, I need to close my eyes again, transcend into dreamless slumber. My daughter's hand encapsulates my own; her touch is cool and silky, not like my own gardener's hands. Her grip is intense and anxious, it is stippled with moisture, and I want to be the one to comfort her, cover her in a protective embrace. I want to make her safe. It's not right to make her feel this way.

At the hospital I stare at the wall, still no blue. The picture on the wall shows an out of date photograph detailing the level of care provided by the seemingly over enthusiastic nursing staff. In the picture, a backcombed horse of a nurse wearing Deirdre Barlow glasses and an artificial smile holds on to an elderly man in a simulated manner.

He seems to strain under her grip, but nobody else has picked up on this, because the picture has gone on the wall anyway, her uniform must be blue, but I don't see it. Though the colour has apparently vanished, there does not seem to be anything in its place, not even grey. Grey is a colour which seems to replace everything at some point or another, grey skies, grey fog, all seems to fade to that all encompassing colour, even us as we progress through life, we develop that greyness. Grey hairs, grey skin, we even begin to wear grey clothes; does that mean our personalities fade to grey too?

I am invaded by a group of young doctors and medics; all fresh and squeaky clean, they probe like human aliens into my brain. They chatter and chirrup amongst themselves, using terminology that sounds like an extra terrestrial language. Conducting test after test, experiment after experiment. Their enthusiasm is overwhelming, almost intoxicating; they shine bright light in my eyes, poke and prod me like a rag doll. I try to tell them about the blue, but the lawn mower noise starts up again, droning its plastic munching racket. They don't respond, just look puzzled, I guess they don't understand either; I am officially trapped in here, confined to my mind, with nobody to talk to but myself.

Eventually the Chief Martian arrives, he seems to be the 'translator', the one in charge, he speaks like he is trying to negotiate his tongue around a particularly large boiled sweet, 'You... have... had... a... stroke... Mrs... Andrews.' It is not until he has finished chewing that I realise the deliberate lingering over his words is for my benefit. 'I am not an idiot' I want to say, but I know it will just be the lawn mower that starts up again, so I remain silent.

My daughter and husband are shown into the cubicle; they have obviously been briefed because my husband has his 'everything is fine' face pasted on, the same face he uses when we have uninvited guests or are in tedious company, it says 'I'm this cheerful all the time,' it looks slightly disturbing if I'm honest, though he would be hurt if I told him. His eyes tell a different story, they say, 'Help me, what am I supposed to do?' He has come straight from work, his tie knot is loosened, top button opened and his shirt sleeves rolled up, his salt and pepper hair looks dishevelled, as though his hand has been raked through it so many times it has lost all sense of direction. He has our daughter in a firm grip, good. I am glad he is here, keeping her safe. She is pale, her rosebud cheeks are ashen and her lips pressed tightly together. She is trying not to cry, to be strong, strong for me. I look into her eyes, I long to see their indigo glaze, but I see nothing. It seems as though my husband is holding both himself and her up, but her arms are gripped firmly around his waist too, they are holding each other together. I have created this mess, this is all my fault.

The first twenty four hours are the worst I have ever known. We are left in a side ward when the Martians and their leader have collected enough samples. A brief though 'matter of fact' speech by a scrub clad duty sergeant about 'over crowding... waiting for a bed... unsure of brain activity... be a few hours' is given to my family. I want to go home, inside I am screaming, 'I'm fine, I just need to get out of here!' I need to let them know that there is nothing wrong with my brain, or the person inside, 'I'm here... I'm inside' I shout, but all they seem to hear is that noise again, that machine-like drone. I want to go home, how can I get through to them? Nothing works, I can't tell them, I can't write it down, and I can't even use sign language, the cord to whatever means I usually use to communicate has been severed by some evil force. I am trapped in a subconscious prison, everyone around me is oblivious to my existence, my soul inside. To them I am lifeless.

I am eventually transported to a ward by two cheerful porters who chat about their weekend plans. They decide who is drinking and who's driving and gossip about who's glad he's single because it means he can pull on Saturday night. They are completely unaware of my silent screams; they look upon me with pity in their eyes. Their uniforms must be blue, I can't make them out. My husband and daughter follow on behind, I see their reflection in a window close by. My daughter looks as though she is walking through my funeral parade; her scrunched up jacket hangs down her folded arms like a wreath. My husband stares straight in front of us, shiny sweat beads form on his furrowed brow, and he swallows hard. He is struggling to keep it together, but he has no choice. I know for him to break now would mean he would never stop breaking.

When we arrive, on the ward I am reminded of that 'Stepford wives' scenario, where the nurses wear compassionate expressions but are careful not to look into my eyes for too long. The ward seems artificially cheerful, with every effort made to create a serene and peaceful atmosphere. I am laced intravenously into a counterfeit countryside. Around me, heart monitors and drip infusers bleat like new lambs in my emerald bedspread field. Tissues used to mop the river falling from my open mouth and stray drips of liquidised breakfast and gooey dinner litter the hospital issue blanket like wild daisies. My sparkling sun is a halogen bulb above my bed, and my family and friends provide a steady stream of plants and flowers to fill my nasal senses with a strange synthetic joy. I am almost outdoors indoors, though the picture is incomplete: without the sky blue walls, everything seems to fade to nothing.

Hours turn into days, days into weeks, still no blue. No sky, no hospital wall, no comfort in my beautiful daughter's eyes. I am held captive in my own body. Eagerly, I await my rescue; I wait for the handsome prince to beat his way through these cataleptic thorns and arrive on his pure white stallion. He will whisk me off to that fairytale land I was in when I woke in the garden. Everything will go back to normal and we will all marvel at my miraculous recovery and I will relay the story every time I am asked. I am determined to fight this. This is not how I will spend the rest of my days; I have too much to do, like travel to distant lands, but before that, and most importantly, I want to experience the delicate cry of my first grandchild.

As I strive through my recovery, I wonder why it is that I have only lost what I have, why this particular colour. I wonder why it is this particular one and not any others. With so much time to think, I can afford to think deeply, analyse, I realise that something that was there before is also lost, without the blue I feel no sadness. I don't feel anything. All the bad things that had gone on in my life before and everything associated with it have shaped what my life has become; it must be that my body was trying to erase it, the colour itself. Now, the 'blues' have disappeared. I can learn to live without the blue; I can concentrate on what I have to gain, on my recuperation. I look to the future, with each day I get stronger and more hopeful. In fact, I realise that I don't even remember what blue is anyway.

I wake one day to feel hot breath on my cheek. Coffee breath, it's my wonderful husband, my devoted husband, they both come every day. He rarely speaks much but we don't need the words, we have learned to communicate through gestures and expressions. 'Wake you did I love? Sorry bout that, you sleep, I'll just sit here and read the paper,' he says. He looks haggard and worn, his shirt is creased and grubby and his face is shadowed with stubble. He needs tidying up, a good scrubbing... he needs me. He has aged ten years in the time I have been away, though for all I know it has been ten years, there is no concept of time here in my solitary confinement. The chair beside my bed has been moved this morning when the nurse gave me a bath, a humiliation I have had to endure since I arrived in this place. I spot the chair and try to raise my shuddering arm in a pointing motion, my arm lifts barely an inch, I splutter and cough under the strain, 'Chaaa' I attempt, the word is muffled with spit but he understands perfectly, 'Thanks love, looking after me again. Don't think you'll ever stop...' His voice fades away into sadness and an agonizing expression seizes his entire face. He seems to hold no hope for me, for normality. But I do, I have nothing else left to hope for.

Movement returns too slowly for me to bear, but... first I am able to lift my arm, then grip a finger, and then hold a pen, but not yet write. In time, I begin to control the lawn mower noise too, I start to form syllables and then words, and I carve my path to my freedom through the nothing. I glimpse my first taste of the real world in what feels like too long to remember.

Physiotherapy begins; it is a series of stopping and starting, coming and going. The same thing, same routine over and over, what I know of the outside world becomes masked in disappointment and repetition. I feel despondent, though I carry on, otherwise I am stuck in that bed; waiting for the next time they will get me out. Outwardly, I make good progress. I indulge their charade so they are pleased with me, I move up their scale to new kinds of therapy, new ways to improve. Soon I am introduced to hydrotherapy, and the effect is magical, I am back in that dream-like state in the garden. Deep in the water I can be enveloped in a silky blanket of cerulean softness, or what I imagine it to be. Delicate bubbles cling to my empty body, they sustain me, allow me to glide inside and out. I am liberated for that short time, open and limitless, though there is no change in my perspective...still no blue, but I don't think I need it anyway. It is slow progress, but I am getting ready to return.

Visiting time again, and my daughter brings the day indoors with her, she is sunshine and rainbows – except without the blue. She tells me about her day, describes even the minute details that don't usually matter, so that I am not missing anything. I can nearly hold her hand in my own now, not like before, in the garden, when she had to hold on to me. The time is never long enough, from the time she vanishes through the swinging doors, back to the reality that awaits her; I am waiting for her to arrive again, counting down. I make sure that I sleep directly after she leaves so that I can hold on to the feeling of her presence for a few more moments. This has taken my freedom, but not my past, not the good times, I can still remember... I remember everything about them. This is why I hold on. She is my life line, the reason I'm not done fighting yet.

Now that I am strong enough, or probably less startling to the outside world, I am integrated with the rest of the ward. My curtains are pulled back and I can see my other bed mates clearly. Five other people just like me, trapped inside themselves, hidden away in imitation sanctuaries where their loved ones can keep them safe. That's not sarcasm, when you cannot speak; you can't say you would rather be anywhere other than here. It's considered the right thing to do, for your own good. Regardless of where your body is, though, you are still encased in your cell. That is something you can only escape from yourself.

They all look like ghosts to me. They are tied up in wires and machinery and appear vacant and disused. Gaunt and lifeless, the only thing alerting anybody to their existence is the occasional moan, cry or twitch. No wonder the nurses are so rigid. Without an unbreakable exterior it would be like running a morgue. This is what I must look like, I am looking in a mirror.

It's another day, but today is different. I don't know why, but somehow I feel renewed hope. I am compelled to do well with my physio exercises, and I have no need to resent that the 'electronically beaming' student nurse feeding me my liquidised lunch has nothing to say to me. I even manage what feels like the beginnings of a weak smile to pass my lips when she has finished and gets up to leave. She is delighted, 'Well, there is no stopping you today Mrs Andrews!' she remarks 'Let's hope it's all downhill from here hey?' I am filled with a new sense of freedom and hope. Today I know will be a good day for me.

As clockwork, my husband arrives on time with his hospital issue lunch bag in his hand. I try to give him the same smile, but with extra conviction, and he bursts with pride. 'Not long now love, it's all going to work out fine,' he says, giving my sunken shoulder a warm and velvety rub. All is as it would be on any other ordinary day; he eats the cheese and pickle sandwich he has picked up in the hospital café at the table beside my bed. He reads me the headlines from the paper, showering my bed with crumbs. He casts the sandwich packaging into the bin and begins to dissect the flapjack he has left, leaving the currants on the side of the paper in a neat pile like a squirrel hoarding for winter. When he gets up to leave, I realise that I don't want him to go, the feeling is over-whelming and he must notice because tears form in his ageing eyes. 'This is not forever love, we won't be doing this for much longer now...' His voice fades to nothing and I can feel the emotion in his touch as he grips my hand so tight I want to cradle him like a child in my arms. 'Don't go... please, today I think I need you to stay,' I want to say... but it's useless. He gathers up what's on the table and turns to leave. As he reaches the swinging doors he turns back and mouths 'I love you' and he is gone.

Later, it is my daughter's turn to arrive. Her usual sun drenched self; she breezes in and showers me with gossip and info. I feel warm and snug in a blanket of reassurance. She plants a loving kiss on my hollow cheek, I lift my eyes to hers... and there it is. That wonderful sensation, I have felt it before, although not for a while now. The feeling intensifies and I can't take my eyes off her, it is drawing me in to her. Entranced by her summer freckle peppered skin, her delicate nose, and rosebud lips. I see her lips move but I don't hear the words. All I can see is her; I can feel her, with those soft golden tresses of hair hanging down to her face, merging into those long, coffee coloured eyelashes bending over her indigo eyes. There it is... I have finally found what is missing, the blue has finally returned to me.

In the far distance, I hear faint noise, an incessant bleeping which gradually begins to die away into one long note. I close my eyes on the blurring bodies drifting closer towards me and I float through my cerulean sky. I am alone in my sapphire sanctuary but for the sound of a lone voice, it could be my daughter... it is, it sounds like she is singing. The song has no words, just one long and entrancing melody. I hear it over and over again, drink in the smell of her sweet perfume. I open my eyes for one final time. She is beside me, where she will always be, and I am immersed in her eyes, they are sparkling and glassy lakes. I take one last shallow breath and I dive in, let all the tropical moisture wash away the pain and the misery that my life has become. I recline in the gentle waves and let them bathe me until I am cleansed and untainted. Now, I am free.

THE AUTHORS

Lucy Delbridge has a degree in theology, but has always preferred writing of a more 'fictional' kind. She gears her MA, and all her other activities, around preparing lunch boxes, making interesting things out of washing up bottles, and changing dirty nappies. As a working mum, much of her free time is focused around her two children, although what time she does have to herself is dedicated to her passions, which are reading anything from a cook book to a literary classic, and her own creative writing. Having written from the time she could actually hold a pen, according to her mother, Lucy is constantly testing her boundaries and likes nothing better than a new challenge.

Katy Griffiths was born and brought up in Pembroke Dock, where reading and writing have always played a huge role in her life. She was an avid reader from a young age and this interest continued throughout her life, culminating in her graduation from Trinity College, Carmarthen in 2007 with a BA in English and creative writing, where she discovered that she could add plays, short stories and a novella to her writing repertoire. She now continues at Trinity College, pursuing the MA in creative writing. Katy draws inspiration from everything and everyone around her, therefore family and friends *could* recognise themselves in her writing. Whether they take that as a compliment or not is up to them!

Caroline James has a long standing interest in writing which goes back to her grandfather reading to her every Saturday on her weekly visit to his house in Gower. Every week she would leave with yet another book underarm to be read before the next visit. Her parents, whilst not wishing to curb her enthusiasm, persuaded her to get a professional qualification and write when she had time. This she did, qualifying first as a criminal lawyer and then taking solicitor's examinations. For a number of years she worked in the Criminal Courts of Cardiff, and is now a consultant. On moving back near to her home town of Swansea she decided to enrol on the MA course full time, concentrating more on writing and less on work. Her aim is to write for the theatre and due to the nature of her job, and her habit of people watching, she is never stuck for ideas. When she has any spare time she enjoys swimming and gardening.

Llinos Jones has been writing intermittently for at least 25 years despite rather rude interruptions by reality. After a break of far too many years she met an unlikely muse (who has borne his burden with grace and good humour) and the words came again. She specialises in free verse but has been known to throw together the occasional sonnet, if pushed. Her poetry has been described as 'sinister yet romantic' and, in fairness, she wouldn't disagree.

Jessie Ledbetter has only had one clear objective in life: to write. Everything else, well, that's just mashed potatoes. Born roughly 9000 miles from Wales, Jessie has always been known for quick, consuming passions and swift, often adventurous decisions. Moving to Los Angeles to pursue the dream job in Hollywood, Jessie stumbled onto the MA creative writing programme at Trinity College when the writers went on strike. Deciding a new life change was in order, Jessie packed a year's worth of a life into two suitcases and made the ten hour flight to the UK. The future is dim and often scary, but Jessie has a few new adventurous ideas in mind and looks forward to hundreds of new experiences, in both the United States and the United Kingdom.

Jo Perkins spends her days wandering along the idyllic sandy beach outside her home in Pembrokeshire or gazing through the windows at the sea searching for inspiration. Actually, that's not true, none of it, except the house which she shares with one husband, three teenagers and three cats, not to mention the stick insect which she would dearly like to see the back of. Sorry, the back of which, she would dearly like to see. Before ending up in this crowded household she acquired an English degree from Swansea and spent many years working as a journalist for BBC TV news.

Jan Slade has been knocking around this world for a long time and she thinks she just might be beginning to understand some of it. She has had a peripatetic life and had many and various jobs, which have all been grist to her writing mill. She now fills her days with reading everything she can get her hands on, allowing her imagination free range with her writing and growing her own vegetables.

What with all these activities she finds she has little time for housework – and what's more, she doesn't care.

Enid M. Smith has been an avid reader from an early age. Lover of trees, the countryside, flora and fauna. She has worked in a variety of jobs before becoming a teacher. She began writing poetry and painting as an emotive teenager. Now she feels it is time to get serious.

Penny Sutton for many years created balance sheets by weaving numbers together. Early widowhood, along with the responsibility of being a single parent to two teenage boys, was the catalyst for exploring her artistic streak. Now in semi-retirement she designs gardens and is close to fulfilling a life long ambition to gain a degree. Too many family tragedies have brought her pen to paper as she grieves with her poetry, avidly supported by her sons and their wives. A lot of her inspiration is drawn from a childhood and married life in several African countries, and is now augmented with the splendour of nature against the backdrop of sky wrapping itself around the lush green Welsh hills. Clouds, the sun and moon, stars and jetliner vapour trails are all clearly visible from her hillside home overlooking the Loughor valley. With so many ideas germinating, she plans to spend more time writing when she retires fully, and being published would be her ultimate triumph.

Sarah Tanner was born in Birmingham, grew up in Herefordshire and spent most of her childhood reading. She started writing when she ten years old, and hasn't stopped since. After completing a degree in English literature and Making It Up As You Go Along – sorry, creative writing – she decided she liked Wales and has remained there ever since. She currently lives in Carmarthen with her house-mates and a yucca plant named Fred. She doesn't like being asked where she gets her inspiration from because, frankly, she has no idea.

MA in Creative Writing

Trinity College Carmarthen

Trinity's MA in Creative Writing is designed for committed writers who wish to complete significant pieces of work and generally broadened their experience as writers.

The workshop programme is run by one of Wales' leading writers, Menna Elfyn. It draws upon a number of adjunct writing staff, and the support of academics experienced in the teaching of all aspects of creative writing.

In addition to the course itself the University supports a number of reading and social events in which you would be able to participate, as well as the publication of a course anthology showcasing students' work.

Study can either be full-time over one year, or part-time over two.

Coleg y Drindod
CAERFYRDDIN
Trinity College
CARMARTHEN

Experience some of Wales' freshest young talent
in this innovative and experimental anthology

Order your copy of *NU* online at:

nuwriting.co.uk

Check the website for more info about *NU*, upcoming event
and how to submit your work for next year's anthology